Sheu y

Saviour

Acknowledgments

To my amazing husband Tel, who inspired me to put pen to paper and write for the first time, thank you for believing in me.

To my children, Lexus, Alicia and Dwayne for all your help in naming my characters; and for all your encouragement whilst I was writing this book, it's helped me out so much.

To my best friend Michelle, you are more of a sister than a friend. Thank you for being one of my biggest fans.

To all my fellow authors and acquaintances in the Twitter Writing Community, thank you for all your advice and connections. It has helped me get to where I am now.

Chapter 1

I was beginning to think I was in the wrong place. I look down at the service sheet. St Mark's Church. It's definitely here.

Something just doesn't seem right. I mean, sure Jemma had her issues but she had more friends and family than this. Why are there so few people here? She was a pillar of the community, a friend to all, someone who would listen to your woes deep into the night without a hint of complaint. That was until she started drinking.

Jemma was my best friend throughout the whole of our lives, from nursery to university. We were inseparable; we studied the same subjects, ate the same foods, and enjoyed the same things, except one thing. I hated horror movies and Jemma loved them, the scarier the better for her.

When we graduated from university, we both moved from our home city of Leeds to the Big City of London. We were so excited! We had interviews at the same law company, we rented a house together, and we were ready to unleash the power of our knowledge on to the city.

We spent the next three years or so working our way up the career ladder, landing big clients and cases but Jemma slowly became a party girl and spent lots of time at the big city clubs and bars. She started to come home in the small hours of the morning, nearly dressed and unable to remember anything from the night before. I tried to talk to her about it, told her she would lose her whole career if she didn't sort herself out.

I covered for her at work just as a best friend would. She was like the sister I never had. I had to look out for her. I was an only child. My parents tried time and again for another baby but it just resulted in miscarriage after miscarriage. My dad was always there for my Mum, maybe that where I learned to look out for Jemma.

Months passed and the nights out got worse. She mixed up two high profile cases in front of the national media. They were so high profile that, if she had been sober, she would have made six figures from one case! The case was taken over by a senior member of our office and Jemma? Well she was fired on the spot. I tried so hard to persuade them to give her another chance and keep her on, but they said 'she was a liability and needed help.' She did. They also said 'she will have trouble finding another job in the city with the reputation she had just given herself.' Meaning she wouldn't get a good reference from them in the future.

So, with her having no job, which meant she didn't have any money to help with the rent and other expenses, she opted to move back to Leeds to be with her parents until she fixed herself up. I was devastated but I understood. I helped her pack up and travelled with her back home. I went to visit my Mum while she settled back in. I couldn't stay long; I had to get back to go over my case notes for my first major solo case. I could get half a million in salary plus bonus if the outcome was right.

I look around at the few people assembled in the church. I can't see her parents. I look again at the start time on the service sheet and realise. I'm half an hour early. I start to relax a little. I'm so glad I haven't drawn any unwanted attention to myself.

I decide to go outside for some fresh air; maybe it will clear my head a little. Just as I turn around I walk into a tall and, quite stocky guy, mumbling my apologies, I take a quick glance upwards. At that instant, it hits me, Liam Smyster, from our Year 9 business studies group at secondary school. He has changed a lot! He was once a shy, slim boy with short fuzzy hair but now he's probably six feet and a bit tall and built like a brick wall. He recognises me straight away. There was me hoping I would have changed enough not to be noticed that quickly, but sadly not.

"Shea, how are you? I must say you haven't aged a bit," he says with half a smile. "I wish we were meeting up under happier circumstances,"

"Hi Liam. I wish I could say I was doing good, but, I don't know, something just doesn't sit right about this," I say, whilst casually shrugging and gesturing to the current surroundings. "Jemma had more friends than this, I'm sure of it."

No one had actually told me how she died. I'd asked countless times, but it seemed to be one big mystery. Something I wasn't allowed to be part of. I tell Liam I would be back in shortly; I needed to breathe for a second before I passed out from thinking too much. It has happened before.

Just as I step outside, I notice the cars and the masses of people; this is starting to feel too real. I walk to greet Jemmas' Mum, recognising her aunts, uncles, and cousins. I'd practised what I would say over and over the whole drive up, but what I had practised didn't seem appropriate. I smile an apologetic smile and give her a brief hug. She whispers how much Jemma loved me and how she spoke highly of me, I smile as a tear slides down my cheek. I watch as they slowly slide Jemmas' white coffin from the Rolls Royce hearse, carried by her father, Derek, her uncles, Charlie and Cecil and 3 extra ushers, I didn't know who they were. I decide to wait until everyone was inside before following along behind.

As I enter the church I can vaguely hear someone whispering my name, I look around frantically. I must look like a crazy woman. I spot Liam signalling that he has saved a seat for me next to him. I make my way, apologetically, past two women who are displaying their displeasure. Taking my seat, I can see Jemmas' Mum quietly weeping at the front. I just want to scoop her up and hold her until she stops. My feet want to move to her side but I don't feel it is my place to be there so I remain seated. I listen as the vicar conducts the ceremony with fluidity and emotion. I haven't really had a chance to read the obituary booklet properly so don't even have a clue who is going to speak. I was asked but politely declined; I didn't think it would be appropriate seeing as though we hadn't spoken properly in a while.

Her cousin, Kevin, steps up first. I knew they weren't close so knew that there couldn't be much for him to say. He kind of babbles on about how Jemma was a bright girl and how she was there for him when they were children, she wasn't, but no one knew except me, no one knew what he had done to her when she was seven. I knew. I knew all her secrets and I swore never to reveal them. And I never have.

So, *'who are you?'* I hear you ask. I'm Shea, a 36 year old solicitor from Leeds, currently living in the big City of London. You could say I'm exactly where I want to be at this point in my life. Well, I say that, what I didn't want to be doing is attending my best friends' funeral.

Although not my first funeral, this one is hurting as much as my Dads. Jemma was with me for that, she was my rock when I was a mess. Jemma held it together for my Mum and me. My Dads funeral was a big affair. With my mixed heritage background, my Dads family travelled long distances to attend it. It lasted hours but was a real insight to his childhood; he never really spoke about it. It was hard to hear how much pain he went through when both of his parents died when he was young. There is still so much to discover. Sometimes I question if I will ever have the time trace my roots. I hope I will have time one day.

Chapter 2

Jemmas' Mum, Harriet, makes her way to the podium next. Her fragile frame shaking with grief, her eyes red and swollen from crying. She walks slowly towards the podium, holding on to the side just to keep her balance. She takes a deep breath, focuses on the Angel at the rear of the church, and speaks about Jemma with a passion I've never heard before.

"Jemma was a gentle soul, one who would gladly put anyone before herself. She studied hard, worked hard, and made her way through life always making hard decisions. She moved away after university to pursue a career in law alongside her best friend, Shea."

At this moment, all eyes were on me. I feel like an animal at the zoo. I was not prepared for this.

"Jemma and Shea were joint at the hip throughout their childhood, sisters, not by blood, but by choice. Shea, please come up and join me," she pleads.

I leave my seat next to Liam and, on shaky feet, take my place next to Harriet.

"I'm sure you all remember Shea. She was practically Jemmas right arm. Keeping her out of trouble, making sure she was studying hard and working harder. Jemma let you down, didn't she Shea?"

"Of course not. Jemma was my best friend, the sister I never had," I croak out. "Jemma was an amazing girl, someone I looked up to, and someone I wanted to be like. I wish I had her confidence." I end with a shaky voice.

I'm not sure where Harriet is going with this speech but I'm starting to get a little worried about what she will say next.

"Jemma had a kind heart and sometimes a brain too fuzzy to realise what was right and wrong but she was always Jemma," Harriet states. "She was OUR Jemma." She finishes with emphasis.

Harriet briefly looks at Jemma's coffin and blows a kiss, all the while holding on to my hand so tight my knuckles turn white. She ushers me off the podium, guides me back to where she is seated, and continues to hold on to me. I'm struggling to work out why she refuses to let go. Maybe I'm the closest thing to Jemma she has besides Derek.

Next up is Belinda; she was in our year at secondary school. She steps up to offer her condolences on behalf of everyone else in our year. It would have been nicer if more than five people had bothered to turn up, but then Jemma and I weren't exactly popular. We kept to ourselves and studied hard. We never wanted to be popular. It seemed to be way too much effort.

Jemmas body is carried away to the instrumental version of Britney Spears' *'Everytime'*. I remember how much she loved the song, always belting it out in the kitchen of our shared house in London. I remember how happy and alive she was. What happened between then and now? What did I miss? I paid so much attention to her and I didn't spot something that a true friend would have.

Once outside the church, Harriet pulls me aside, away from everyone else. She pulls me in for a hug but this isn't just a normal hug.

"Someone killed her Shea," Harriet whispers.

"What?" I demand.

"Hush child, and listen. I need you to meet me tomorrow, at the little cafe near to your mother's house. There are some things I need you to see, but I can't show you at our house, it has to be there. Be there at 10am, please?" she begs.

"I'll be there, but Harriet, this is so strange. You should go and be with your family. Be sure to rest and I will see you tomorrow." I hug her hard and place a kiss on her cheek.

The thought from before came back to slap me in the face. I knew something wasn't right about this!

My Mum notices, almost instantly, that something is wrong. I could tell by the look she gives me, that 'sympathy without speaking' look. I smile sweetly and give her a hug. Mum had left the church before I did. She had gone back home and freshened her make-up and re brushed her hair, ready for the wake.

"I'm alright Ma," I say softly.

"Maybe you are, but you might want to explain that to your face darling," she says.

My Mum is the most amazing but most sarcastic woman I know, besides myself, obviously. She has been by my side through thick and thin and I guess you could say she has also been my rock. After Dad died, I had to be there for her, hold her whilst she cried her broken heart out, glue her back together with happy memories of Dad, and his 'dad jokes' the ones that made him cry with laughter, they made absolutely no sense but we laughed with him. I would remind her that he is always with her, through life and death. He would always be there to guide her through the rest of her life without actually being here. It's been hard and we've been through rough patches but we've always emerged out the other side smiling.

"Mum?" I ask, "Have you and Harriet had lunch or met up at all since Jemma passed?"

"Maybe just the once sweetheart, why do you ask?" she replies quizzically.

"I'm worried about her, that's all Mum," I reply, still worried about what Harriet had told me earlier.

"You have always been worried about someone," she says with a giggle, "You are a born worrier!"

"I blame you Mum," I beam, "I take after you on so many levels."

"You have your Fathers ways too honey," she says as she turns away and swipes at a tear.

The wake is a small affair, only a handful of people have bothered to turn up. Harriet and Derek make small talk with the guests who attended before everyone slowly filters away. The hall is decorated in Jemmas' favourite colours, burgundy and purple. I always said she was slightly colour blind. There are pictures of her from her childhood scattered around, even some from our outings in London. I notice there aren't many from her later years. I need to find out what happened to her. Tomorrow can't come quick enough.

Mum and I sit for dinner later that evening, talking about my job, how I hadn't made her a Grandma yet, and how she desperately hoped I would find someone special soon. We laugh about old times, reminisce about Dad, joke about how she had never learnt to change a light bulb herself or how to change the fuse in the plug. She would always call for Louis down the street. His wife and Mum are really close, have been for many years. I think, after Jemma and I left for London, Harriet and Mum drifted apart. I never did work out why. I regret that I didn't really keep in contact with Jemma much after she came back home. I hate myself for that. I had so much going on that after a few months I just didn't reach out. I never updated my social media accounts with anything new. If I had just stayed in contact, maybe she would have told me what was happening. I could have helped her. I could have saved her. I am THE worst friend ever.

I wake early the next morning; sweating from the dream I had the night before. I quickly write it down in my Dream Diary, something I'd been keeping for the past two years, mainly because I'd been having some unsettling dreams and they were very vivid.

'I'm running through the wet grass, looking back every now and then to see if he's still there. I can't see him though. I can hear him, panting and breathing heavily behind me. I don't know who he is or even what he looks like. I've never even seen his face; all I hear is his breathing. He's getting closer. I can sense him behind me; I duck behind a gigantic tree, trying to control my breathing. I see his shadow, slowly creeping up on me. He walks slowly, scanning behind the trees around me. I flatten myself to the floor, trying to blend in as much as I can. I slow my breathing down enough to hold it for a minute. He looks directly at me without actually seeing me. He looks so innocent, yet so familiar. Just before I can recognise him, I wake up, sweating.'

I take a quick shower, mainly to wake myself up a little. I can smell bacon. The smell works its way through the house. I dress quickly in something light; I can feel the temperature rising already and its only 8:30am. I tame my hair into an afro pony on the top of my head and make my way down to the dining room. Mum has made a mountain of breakfast, enough to feed the entire street and then some. I'm not feeling that hungry but she has made so much effort, how could I refuse?! Mum turns around so fast she catches the surprised look on my face before I can change it to a smile. She quickly says she has invited Louis and his wife, Lana, for breakfast too and at that moment there is a knock at the door.

I quickly answer it to the smell of freshly baked cookies. Lana always makes the best choc chip cookies in the town, and she knew they were my favourite. She stepped through the door and threw her arm around me.

"Oh Shea!" she says softly. "How are you feeling darling?"

"I'm doing alright Lana, thank you for asking. Your cookies haven't changed their smell." I manage without my voice cracking.

"Ah well, your Mum mentioned you were coming back for poor Jemmas funeral, I knew I had to do something for you," she purrs. "I'm sorry we couldn't make it to the funeral honey. Louis and I were travelling back from Northampton after visiting Louis's parents."

"It's OK Lana. I'm just glad to have been given the time off to attend myself. My boss's boss is a nightmare, especially with such a high profile case coming up soon," I say.

I thank her again with a big hug and quickly proceed to acknowledge Louis with a hug. They step past me and into the dining room. Just as I turn to close the door, I see him. The man from my dream.

Chapter 3

I must have looked a fright when I returned because everyone was staring at me. Mum rushes to sit me down, I can hear her saying something about looking as pale as a ghost and how I must be low on vitamins. Typical of Mum to blame vitamins, everything was vitamins this and vitamins that. I took extra when I was younger just to make her happy. I sit for a few moments before a cup of strong, sugary tea was thrust into my hands. Louis smiles sweetly when I look up at him but he doesn't utter a single word. He had done exactly what my dad would have done in that situation. Dad believed tea fixed everything. He was probably right in his own way but I knew that tea wasn't going to fix this or even prepare me for what I was about to find out from Harriet. I glance at the clock and notice how close to 10am it was. I quickly excuse myself and plant a kiss on everyone's forehead; I believed they deserved that after I nearly passed out on them all.

I meet Harriet at the cafe as planned. Before I can sit down, I notice the size of the folder she has on the table. I had folders of coursework and university work but this was a whole other level of fullness. I sit down opposite her but she looks preoccupied with something behind me. I turn, just slightly, to see the same guy again. This is starting to get a little weird. That's twice in the same morning and judging by the look on Harriet's face, this isn't the first time she had seen him either and this worries me even more.

She quickly grabs the folder and my arm and drags me off towards the church, whispering quickly that he wouldn't follow us there. I am genuinely getting concerned about our safety and her sanity. This man has been in my dreams for the past two years and now he is in my home city. Could I really be losing my mind? At 36? Early onset dementia? I'm too confused to think straight.

We plough through the church doors, apologising to the vicar for disturbing his morning sermon. Taking seats at the back of the church, Harriet quickly opens the folder, trying to get everything out in one breath.

"Jemma was having dreams, something out of the ordinary, and something that made her wake up screaming, and in terrible sweats, she would call out for you Shea. Cry blue murder that he was too close to you, that he could smell your fear, that he could sense your movements," she says frantically.

"OK, take a breath Harriet. What dreams and how long had she been having them?" I ask, slowly.

"Two years! Two very long years before I found her one morning, in her bed, unresponsive and covered in....oh!" she weeps silently.

"Harriet?" I try to steady my voice, "Was Jemma killed in her sleep?" I ask softly, my voice shaking..

"Oh Shea, she was calling out to you night after night. Howling tears like I've never seen before. Something or someone spooked her. Either in her dreams or in reality, but Shea, you have to read this folder. Everything she ever wrote about it, is inside." She says, as she shoves the folder into my hands.

I take the folder with shaky hands. I'm going to need somewhere quiet to even begin to read what is inside. Am I even prepared for it all? What would I do with the information? I doubt the police would even believe something about dreams. Most normal people don't believe in them. I didn't. Up until I started having really vivid ones. I guess I will just have to find out what hers were about, but from what Harriet has said, they sound a lot like my own. That could only mean one thing, well, I think it could, it's something we have experienced together.

It's been so long since I've been to Leeds; I've almost forgotten where all the best peaceful places are. The library? Maybe a quiet table at the local Costa; no, for some reason, my feet take me to the gates of the cemetery.

I guess they know best. I won't be disturbed here. Hardly anyone likes these places, they steer well clear unless they have no choice of course. Anniversaries of loved ones deaths, birthdays of the lost and indeed the funerals of those we hold so dear. This isn't my favourite place either, but I feel closer to Jemma by being here. Maybe I can understand her notes better here. Don't get me wrong, I'm not one to believe in ghosts and the spirit world but I can't ignore the fact that my feet brought me here for a reason and that seems to be the only logical one!

I find the bench that is furthest from the entrance. I know I will be well hidden from prying eyes. I'm still holding the folder so close to my chest that my arms are starting to lose circulation. I open the folder to the first entry, if that what you could call it. A scrap of paper with my name almost scratched into it. In all manners of colours and fonts. Graffiti and bold, italic and script, it's almost scary that Jemma could even write in this way. I've never seen it in the 30 plus years we had been friends. I question if I'm really reading something Jemma wrote. As I turn through the pages, I notice the swirls she gives her S's and the tails she gives her Y's and J's. I know, now, that this is Jemmas work.

'He won't leave me alone, chasing me through my dreams. I've seen him around town. He's out for Shea; he won't stop until he catches her.'

This is a whole new level of scary. How could she be having the same dreams as me, about the same person, if it truly was the same person? I turn a few more pages and something catches my eye. She's drawn an almost exact sketch of the same man I've seen twice today and the exact outline I've been seeing in my dreams for the past two years in my dreams! She really was seeing the same person, but how? Can the same person really be in two people's dreams at the same time at over 300 miles apart? Was he real or a spirit? A spirit, really Shea? What are you thinking?

I close the folder on the sketch. Just then, I glimpse something out of the corner of my eye. Did I really just see something or am I just really tired and need some proper sleep? These past two years have been diabolical on my sleep pattern; I'm surprised I manage to keep up at work! I decide to take the folder back to Mums, get some rest, and then check everything over later. Luckily, I carry my sleep diary everywhere so I can cross reference everything she saw with what I saw. I think I may have to start a day diary if this person has managed to escape dreamland!

Chapter 4

I can hear raised voices coming from Mum's living room as I open the front door. I can single out Mum's voice clearly. The other three, not quite as easily. I open the adjoining door as quickly and quietly as I can to assess the situation before I decide to join in but I am dumbfounded to find the police arguing with Mum! Just to mention, we've never had any trouble with the police, so to find them arguing with Mum in her own living room has me speechless. I open my mouth to speak just as the taller of the two men turns, his face pales. He looks like he had seen a ghost, poor fella!

Mum turns to me, then back to the shorter, stumpier man and says, "I told you it wasn't her!"

"Would you mind having a seat at the table?" he asks me with a shaky voice. He is still trying to sound official and in charge, but something has shaken him up.

I sit down, ready for a barrage of questions, probably about the folder and its contents. I'm not sure who else knows about it. I place my bag on the table and look at him as he sits, carefully on the chair next to me. He swallows loudly, as if trying to summon the vocal power to ask the next question.

"May I ask," he starts, "Where you have been for the past four hours?" he finishes finally.

"I've been at the cemetery. I also met with Harriet Summers at the cafe, six doors down, why do you ask?" I question.

"We have had a report of the body of a young lady in the alleyway next to Tesco," he replies.

He digs inside his jacket pocket for his phone. Still watching me closely. He brings up a picture of the girls face. I nearly lose my breakfast. This

girl is almost my double, right down to the birthmark on my neck, just a small mark, the size of an ant, on the ride side of my neck, just below my earlobe.

I start to hyperventilate, trying to make sense of everything in my head before I even try to say anything to this man. The police officer, who has already shown this picture to my Mum and probably, almost certainly, given her a heart attack, just watches me, no offer of a drink of water! But, how had Mum known it wasn't me? It's like, she was certain it wasn't me, but I guess that is parents in general, unless proven otherwise they won't believe it. Who could this poor girl be and why is she dead?

I ask the officer if I can see the picture again, maybe it will jog a memory of a passerby. As I study the picture, as closely as I dare to look, I can see the emptiness in her eyes. Whoever did this to her stole her soul. They took her future away from her. Someone or something did the same to Jemma. It's now up to me to search for the answers. I feel like I'm the only one who can. I rarely say that I don't trust the police, but I can't imagine the comments they would make.

I finally notice the third person, standing quietly in the shadows. Yvette Mundane. This girl, although the same age as me, presides to look down her nose at me, in the living room of my own mother. Her raven black hair trailing down her back, tied tightly in a neon orange scrunchie. Two hair grips either side of her forehead, obviously there to hold some sort of fringe back in place.

"Why are you here?" I ask dominantly.

"I heard raised voices and thought your Mum might have needed some help," she answers snootily.

"Well, I'm here now so you can leave, thank you for coming over," I relay, with as much politeness as I can muster at this precise moment.

She turns on her heel, throws me a look of disgust and walks out. I can't believe the number one bully in our school thought she had the right to look down her nose at me after all these years. She bullied

Jemma all the time, about her hair style, the fact she had acne and the fact her clothes weren't 'top brand' names. No one else cared. Only Yvette. She had to be one or two better than everyone else.

Glancing back at the photo on the officers' phone, I commit the picture to memory as best I can. I guess it would have been easier to just look in the mirror, only this girl had deep blue eyes, something very rare in our heritage. This poor girl had her life stolen. She looks too much like me for it to be a coincidence. I'm terrified and it shows. Mum looks scared; she grabs my hand and begs me to tell her what's wrong. This is going to be a very long and very tiring night. We will need lots of tea and maybe a treat of a takeaway. I don't think either of us is in the mood to cook anything.

After promising to inform the police if anything strange happens through the night, they leave apologetically. I take a moment to scan the street for anyone lurking around who shouldn't be, but all is quiet. I close and lock the door behind me, something Mum has never really had to do before tonight. Between Mum and me, we decide to order a huge supply of Chinese. I gather the folder and my sleep diary and start setting up the table for our lengthy discussion about everything. I hadn't mentioned my dreams to anyone, least of all my Mum. She would have insisted that I come home so she could look after me. She was the ultimate carer but also, the ultimate worrier, this is where I get it from! I knew I had to tread carefully when explaining everything to her.

I jump out of my skin when the doorbell rings. I must have been daydreaming. I use the spy hole in the door to see who it is. I recognise him straight away. I open the door.

"Shea. What a surprise to see you! I'm sorry to hear about poor Jemma," he says solemnly.

"Thank you Lin. How is your lovely wife? Still smiling I hope!" I reply sweetly.

"Oh yes," he beams, "She's 74 now and never stops smiling. I will tell her you asked after her."

"Thank you. Have a great evening." I say as I pay my money and wave him off.

They are such a lovely family. I'm glad they still own the place. I take the food into the dining room where Mum had just placed the teapot on the table. I haven't seen it since Dad died. This chat will take more than just one cup so the teapot is needed. We make minor chit chat while dishing out the food between us. When the final box is empty, we make a start. I know how hard this is going to be so I prepare Mum.

"Mum, you have to promise to listen with an open mind," I begin.   "This is hard for me to explain and I know it will be hard to hear."

"I'm all ears darling," she said. "Everything you say will remain within these 4 walls."

"It started just over two years ago, just before Jemma returned home." I take a deep breath. I open my sleep diary to the first entry, 7th August 2017.

Chapter 5

7th August 2017- Shea

'Jemma went out again last night. I'm really worried about the amount she drinks. She seems to never stop. I've tried to speak to her about it but she is adamant that she can handle it; she says I'm 'mothering' her. I'm sure her Mum would do more than tell her to stop drinking! She would take the drink and throw it all over her! Harriet didn't like alcohol. Says it's the devils drink. She's probably right.

On a different note, I had a really strange dream last night. I woke up this morning sweating like I had been running a marathon. A man is chasing me; I don't even know who he is or why he is chasing me. I wish I could find some answers. I can't even speak to Jemma about this, I've tried to talk to her about work but she just doesn't seem to want to listen. She seems hell bent of drinking her life away. I hope I can sleep better tomorrow. There's a huge case coming up and I can't mess this up.'

I show Mum the first entry to my sleep diary. Mum reads it with a sparkle in her eyes, almost like she agrees with what I've written.

"You're not wrong there darling," she laughs, "Harriet would drown her in it just to make sure she never touched it again."

"You're probably right Mum. Jemma said what her Mum didn't know wouldn't hurt her." I reply.

I quickly take the folder out to see when Jemma started writing her entries. She started on the 7th August too. This is way too much to take in. We were best friends, like sisters. Our birthdays were only 1 day apart. We liked most of the same things, plus we started a diary on the same day without the other knowing. Too much of a coincidence? I think so. I quickly check the time. 8:45pm. Harriet would still be awake. I need to ask her something very personal.

I dial Harriet and wait.

"Hello?"

"Hi Derek, its Shea" I say.

"Shea, sweetheart. How are you?" He asks.

"I'm good thank you. Is Harriet around at all?" I ask.

"Just a second honey," he says as he covers the mouthpiece to shout for his wife.

"Hello Shea, what's wrong? Harriet asks worriedly.

"Harriet, can I ask you something personal?" I ask very carefully.

"Of course, go right ahead" she replies.

"Please excuse me for asking but were you both trying for a baby when you fell pregnant with Jemma?" I ask with a hint of embarrassment.

"Oh!" She laughs, "I do excuse you for that!" She still has a hint of laughter in her voice. "We were surprised to find out about Jemma. Mainly because we were told we would never have children, so we just thought the doctors must have been wrong before and that it wasn't our time until then" she finishes.

"I'm really worried Harriet," I start, "We were born one day apart, we like all the same things and now, I find out we started diaries on the same night, without a hint to each other." I finish.

The line goes deathly quiet for what seems like an eternity.

"Well that does sound strange Shea," she says, finally.

"I'm going to dig a little further into this. I will keep you informed Harriet. Try to rest and give Derek my love." I end the call.

Something is really weird with this. I don't know exactly how this all fits in to place or even if any of this is relevant to what's happening now, but maybe I'll look up on it. Could the doctors have been wrong when they told Harriet she couldn't have children? It's been known, right? It sets my mind wandering for a few moments.

Landing back into reality with a bump, I go back to Mum. I've left her alone long enough for her to get herself into trouble!

Mum is flicking through Jemma's folder when I return to the room. She's holding the sketch in her hand while reading something on a small scrap of paper.

"What have you found Mum?" I ask trying not to startle her.

"Oh just something about this sketch," she replies. "Something Jemma has written is ringing some bells."

"Do you recognise him?" I ask hopefully.

"He does look familiar honey, but I just can't think why," she says, putting the sketch down on the table.

She picks up the teapot to pour herself another cup. I look away for a brief second before I hear the smash. I turn back to find the teapot on the floor and Mum shaking like a massage chair on high speed.

"What is it Mum?" I ask hurriedly.

"I've....I've just seen the man from the sketch," she manages to say. "He...he was in the garden!"

Now I'm convinced I'm not going insane if Mum has seen him too! How do I explain seeing him in my dreams as well as in reality?

I sit Mum down with another cup of tea. Dads' speciality, strong and sugary. She's still shaking. I venture into the

garden, just to check he isn't still lurking behind the shrubbery. The garden is clear except for the local hedgehog family. I think they've been here since I was a child. We would always watch as the little babies scurried after their mother across the grass. I go back into the house but keep checking behind me. As I sit back at the table with Mum, I open Jemma's diary. It feels wrong to be reading it but I have to find out what was going on.

7th August 2017 – Jemma

'Shea has been complaining about me going out again. Why doesn't she come with me one night? She will see how fun it is. The club is amazing, full of different people. It's so much better than sitting in the house looking over case notes every night. When we moved here, I expected it to be fun, but it's just constant work. Shea doesn't even want to try to

have fun. She's changed from the outgoing girl at university. Maybe she will change soon. It just takes time.

I had a dream last night. I was in a dark forest somewhere. It was damp and horrible. I could hear someone running. They were getting closer to me, but then I caught a glimpse of, what I thought was Shea. Why would she be in my dream? He ran past me, heading straight for her. I woke up before I saw anything else. I hope I don't dream that again.'

I can't believe what I'm reading. It is almost the same as mine. Something else stands out to me. Jemma described me as an outgoing girl at university but I only went to three parties over the whole four years! Or could it be because I was outspoken? It has to be that, because I always tell people what I think of them whether they like it or not, that must have been what she was meant. I check in on Mum, but she had decided to turn in to bed after that cup of tea, she had left a little note saying that the events of the night had given her a bit of a headache. I feel exactly the same.

With Mum sleeping soundly, I make my way to the living room, settle on the pale blue fabric sofa, stuffed full of cushions and continue through the folder. There are page after page of diary entries, scraps of paper with sketches of wooded areas and shadowy figures. A few of the wooded areas look familiar but then I guess one wooded area could look the same as a million others. Most of the sketches look so familiar to my dreams, but how could we be having the same dreams? Was it even possible? I reach for my laptop to do some research.

I open up Google and type 'can two people dream the same dream at the same time?' I check the time whilst I wait for the results. 11:35pm, wow where did the time go? Ah results…brilliant! So, according to these results it IS possible. Normally for mother and daughter, best friends and partners without even forward planning or conversation about the dream, it says that forward planning for this to happen is dangerous. No statement as to why though...interesting! I make a mental note to check up on it later. Jemma and I never spoke about our dreams or diaries. This is just too much for me tonight, if I don't get some sleep I will officially become a zombie! I'm too terrified to sleep but I have to.

'He's coming again, I can hear his footsteps, faster and closer they get, I can almost feel his breath on my neck. I just need to turn to see who or what he is. I quickly flatten myself against the tree.

"Come on Shea, just a quick look," I say to myself.

Deep breath and look!

I come face to face with my nightmare tormentor!'

I wake up sweating, still lying on the sofa, with Mum knitting in the chair next to me, silently watching the morning talk show.

I glance at the clock that hangs above the mirror, that takes pride of place above the fireplace.

"Mum, it's almost 10:30am why didn't you wake me up?" I ask.

"Oh, I tried darling. You told me to leave you alone so I did," she said softly.

"Did I say anything else when I was asleep?" I dare myself to ask.

Mum is mesmerised by the TV.

"Sorry dear, what did you say? I was engrossed in the news about that young girl from yesterday. You remember? The one on that policeman's phone," she says with a tear in her eye.

"I asked if I said anything else, but don't worry about that now, what have they found out?" I ask.

"They say her name was Sierra Jackson, she was just barely twenty-one. Her Mum said she was studying Law at university." Mum relays with a new sadness in her voice, something I hadn't heard before. I can see her tears silently falling with the thought of how Sierra's Mum is feeling. For the first time, I don't even know what to say to my Mum. I gently squeeze her shoulder as I leave the room; she pats my hand blindly not taking her eyes off the television.

I run upstairs for a shower to wash the patches of sweat away. I feel like I've been swimming in a swamp! I let the water wash over me while I go back over what I saw in my dream. The dark eyes, the stark white of his skin compared to the darker complexion of mine. His hair is the brightest red I've seen, but this isn't the same man I've seen around town, the man Harriet and Mum have seen, could it be a different man in each of our dreams? This man doesn't look anything like Jemma's sketch. Could I have assumed they were the same person just because everything we did growing up was the same?

I go downstairs, deciding to leave my hair loose and wild today. There's a first for everything! I always tie my hair up.

I pick up the sketch that Jemma drew. This guy has dark eyes and a darkish skin tone with dark hair, so we could be seeing different men. If we have, or were, then why does this sketch cause such a reaction for me, a sense of knowing? Then it hits me like a shovel in the face....I know him...Personally!

Chapter 6

I open up my laptop again to access my case files via the Cloud, amazing piece of work this! I'm sure there is a picture of him in here somewhere.

Jemma and I worked his case just over two years ago. He was on a charge of child abduction and assault of a woman. We were prosecuting him.

Ah! Here it is! Case Number CAA460. Jack Woodwin. He struck me as odd from the first time I read what he had done.

Case Number CAA460.

Name: Jack Woodwin.

Age: 41

Location: Vauxhall, London.

Charges: 1 count of Child Abduction

        1 count of Assault.

Case Description: Defendant, Jack Woodwin, abducted Annalise Shaw from her school playground at 3:15pm on Tuesday 9th May 2017. He proceeded to take her to an old abandoned factory near to the old Battersea Power Station, where he held her for 3 days awaiting a payment from her family of £15,000. The family raised the money and paid him but they had the police on standby at the drop point. The mother went to drop the money off only for Mr Woodwin to proceed to assault Mrs Shaw. Injuries include a fractured jaw and left eye socket, minimal damage to limb ligaments and radial fracture to left wrist. Annalise suffered mental trauma, no physical injuries stated.

Notes: Defendant pled guilty to abduction and assault. Trial set for 31st July 2017.

I remember the date well. It was a warm day, not too humid, with a light breeze. The sun was mid way through the sky; Jemma wore a black knee length skirt with court shoes, a white blouse and black blazer. Her makeup was as natural as it could be for her. Her hair in a tight bun atop her head. I wore something similar but in navy blue with diamond stud earrings. My face, naked of makeup, and my hair in a high afro-pony. We walked into the courtroom with high spirits; positive we could win and obtain a custodial sentence.

When we arrived we were escorted to a side room and given the worst news possible.

Jack had obtained false documents whilst out of bail and had fled the country.

I remembered the way Jemma looked, like the life had been ripped from her. I assured her that the police would find him and bring him back to face justice. How wrong was I? He was never traced. The police said they checked all the CCTV from airports and ferry terminals, there wasn't a glimpse of him anywhere. I figured he would change his image just to avoid being spotted. I didn't expect him to change this much.

When I last saw him he had short stubbly hair, brown, if I'm correct, and greyish colour eyes. He was a stocky build and medium height. Judging by Jemmas' sketch, and from what I've noticed in the street. He now has, what looks like, shoulder length brown hair and dark brown eyes. He looks like he has lost some of the weight or maybe just toned himself up a little. Just then something else pops into my head. I saw another person in my dream last night. There was a third person. Someone in the background. They had stark white hair that stretched down to their waist, with turquoise colour eyes. It stuck with me because it is such a sight to see. As much as I hate these dreams, I'd secretly love to find out who that one person is.

"What are you doing Shea darling?" Mum says.

"I've finally worked out who the guy from my dreams is Mum!" I imply, half excitedly, half cautiously.

"Oh?" She questions, "Who is it?"

"Jemma and I were the prosecutors in his child abduction/assault case back in 2017," I reply, "He skipped the country while out on bail a few days before his trial, but he's never been located."

"But honestly, if that's the conclusion, how did he get into your dreams and more importantly, how did he get back out?" Mum asks.

"That's where I'm trumped Ma," I reply defeatedly

I load up my laptop and open the internet search page when the doorbell rings.

Realising Mum has managed to evade me and leave the house via the back door; I get up from the dining table to open the door. I put the chain in place before opening it, maybe I'm being childish but I'm still jittery. As I open the door slightly, someone is pushing it from the other side.

"Come on Shea, hurry! Let me in!"

It's Harriet and she sounds worried or upset, or both.

"Just a second," I call out.

Removing the chain, she practically falls through the door and just manages to regain her balance before hugging the floor.

"What's the emergency?" I ask, side stepping slightly to avoid the door from hitting me in the face.

"He's watching the house." She manages, through deep breaths.

"Sorry, who?" I ask, probably not wanting to know but I'd already asked.

"The man from the sketch!" She replies in a hushed voice, "How did he get here?"

"I was about to try and find out," I manage to say in between her interruptions.

I go back to the table with Harriet at my heels, How do I even start this search? Should I just type, 'people from dreams in reality' or 'can people travel from dreams into the real world?' I really don't know how to start. Harriet puts the kettle on for some tea, but I know I'm going to need something a little stronger for this.

"Harriet, stay here, I'm just going to the shop, and I will NOT be long. I will pick us up some of that chocolate that you like," I call out as I reach for my denim jacket.

"Oh, are you sure that's wise dear?" she calls from the kitchen.

"It will be all right Harriet. Lock the door behind me if you feel the need, but you are safe here," I reply with care in my voice.

"OK dear. I will do!" Harriet calls again. I can hear cupboards opening and closing as I leave the house the same way Mum had done not long ago! I wonder where she had gone.

I make my way to Tesco, having left Harriet in my mothers' kitchen. I'm not sure that was a good idea now, she's probably making a cake or something. It does help her calm down though. I search for Mum along the way, but I don't see her anywhere. On my way there, I remember where the police said they found Sierra and made a mental note to buy some flowers for her and also trace her parents to send a condolence card from me and Mum.

I browse Tesco for some snacks and a bottle of white wine for the long research day ahead. I pick up some cookies, crisps and Harriets favourite chocolate, Galaxy Caramel, and a bottle of Chardonnay. I don't drink very often so I know this will last me a while. I buy some bright flowers to leave at the scene of Sierras' death; I sign the card from Mum and me. I then recognise Yvette standing a few places in front of me in the queue. I really don't think I can put up with her smarmy remarks right now so I turn to try and hide behind the man in front of me.

"Shea? Is that you?" I hear.

Dammit to high heavens, she spotted me!

"Oh, Hi Yvette, I didn't see you there," I reply.

"I almost didn't recognise you with your hair like that!" She states, pointing at the wildness of my afro. "You normally have it up!"

"Well it's nice to make a change once in a while!" I say through gritted teeth.

"I see you have a lovely bottle of Char there!" She points out, "The tragic death of Jemma must be turning YOU to drink now. You two never did anything different so it must be hard for you to be by yourself now," she giggles with her friend like we are still five years old.

I try not to lower myself to her level so I give her 'food for thought', as my Mum would say.

"At least I had a best friend one who was loyal," I smile, glancing sideways at the girl she was with, "Have a nice day!"

I turn away as a single tear falls from my eye. I don't actually think its hit me that Jemma is truly gone and is never coming back.

I pay for my shopping and turn left after leaving the shop. As I turn, I see some other people placing flowers at the scene so I go out to join them, mainly so I didn't look odd placing them there by myself. As I get closer, I can see a couple holding each other, looking distraught. I quietly place the flowers and card down, and mentally utter a prayer. In no way am I hugely religious, but a quiet prayer now and then doesn't harm anyone.

The lady of the couple turns to acknowledge me and her face drains of all colour. Ah! This must be Sierras' parents. Dammit all to the ground!

"'I'm so sorry for your loss Mr and Mrs Jackson," I say softly.

"You look so much like her, how can it be?" Mr Jackson says.

"I honestly can't answer that sir." I say solemnly. "If you don't mind me saying so, you don't sound like you are from the Leeds area."

"No, not really," Mrs Jackson replies quietly. "We moved here from Oxford, just six months or so ago."

"It may sound useless, but I hope you decide to stay. I would really like to stay in contact, I feel as if this is all my fault. I don't know why at the moment, maybe because she looks so much like me, but I will figure it out." I offer up with a smile.

"I don't think we would be able to leave even if we wanted to now, this is Sierras' last known place. We would love to stay in contact also, thank you, but please do not blame yourself. You weren't to know what was going to happen, otherwise, you wouldn't be here. Also thank you for the flowers. I really hope the police find who has done this to our girl," Mrs Jackson finishes with a gentle intake of breath.

We exchange contact details, including my Mums address and part ways. During the walk back, something clicks in my head. Why would anyone attack Sierra? Something is off with this. First Jemma dies, and then someone attacks a girl who looks like me. Could this someone have been after me? Could Jack be stalking us? If he has seen Jemma here, he must assume I'm here too. I've now made myself feel even guiltier. I could be the reason that Sierra is dead. Great! Well done Shea!

When I get back to Mums, I can hear her and Harriet talking together. Harriet mustn't have locked the door after all. It reminds me of the old days when they would always be in each other's kitchens, if they weren't complaining about the weather or us kids, they were complaining about how Dad and Derek were working all hours, never being able to spend time together but they always said how much loved their husbands. I open the door to the kitchen slowly and take in the scene before me. I smile from deep in my heart and telepathically tell Jemma how good it is to see them together again. I clear my throat to announce my return.

"Where did you pop off to?" Mum asks.

"I could ask you the same thing," I laugh. "I just went to Tesco Mum, I fancied something a little stronger than tea," I say, pulling out the bottle.

"Ooh! I'll get the good glasses!" She says, opening the cupboard, avoiding my question like a pro.

"I'll stick with this," says Harriet, holding up her cup of tea.

"Of course," I smile, remembering how she is not a fan of alcohol. I throw her a huge bar of chocolate and watch as she smiles like a Cheshire cat.

As Mum places the 'good' glasses on the dining table, the glasses that haven't been touched since the last Christmas with Dad. I gather my things from the living room floor, ready to begin my research. I settle my laptop, Jemma's folder and my diary on the table. I, then, update Harriet on how I worked out who the man in the sketch is most likely to be. She doesn't believe what I'm saying at first, but when I pull up a picture of Jack that I found online, she almost dropped her tea!

"Oh my, it does look like him, but there is a lot of differences sweetie" she says.

"I know, but he still has the same features. You see how his eyes droop down at the corners?" I say, whilst pointing at both the sketch and the laptop screen.

She agrees but is finding it hard to work out the whole dreaming aspect, and she isn't alone with that.

"So, if he's a real person, excuse the Pinocchio pun how is he in both of your dreams and why on Earth is he chasing you both?" Mum demands to know.

"That's what I'm working on Mum," I reply with a smile.

"Oh honey, I'm sorry. It's just so scary to think what he could be capable of," she says, giving Harriet a comforting look.

"I know Mum, that's why I'm looking into it," I smile at them both.

I quickly fill them in on meeting Sierra's parents and how I'm convinced Jack is looking for me. If it was him who attacked Sierra that is. I also told them what Yvette had said in the shop. How Jemma and I were never apart so I must be taking things badly. It had made me feel guilty that I wasn't there to protect her. Harriet and Mum gave me warm hugs, which made me feel a little bit better, still guilty though.

"There wasn't anything anyone could have done to stop her Shea. I tried every trick in the book, in every book!" Harriet told me as she held my face in her hands. "Jemma was stubborn! Just like her Mama!"

I laughed a little at her last statement. Harriet really was stubborn, but it was a good thing. It's just a shame Jemma had inherited that trait from her mother and not the calmness and softness of Derek. She would have knocked the drinking on the head a long time ago had she been like her father. He and Dad were alike in many ways. That's what made them such good friends.

Chapter 7

I open up my notepad and attempt to start a timeline, starting from the date we were given the case. I work forward from there adding in any other little bits of information along the way, from strange sightings listed in

Jemma's diary and notes, to odd letters Jemma found, to the death of Sierra. To the untrained eye, it just looked like a spiders' web, a very drunk spiders' web!

I explain the whole thing to Mum and Harriet; I point out all the dates and explain their meaning to the line. I look through Jemma's folder to see if there is anything else to add, and, boy, did Jemma have plenty! Harriet looks over my shoulder whilst I read a handwritten note left for Jemma from Jack.

Dear Jemma,

Do you remember me? I BET YOU DO! Do you remember trying to send me to jail? You and your friend. Well you didn't win! You both ruined everything for me! You will both pay for it. You, Jemma, will be the easiest. You don't watch your back when you out, you're not as cautious as your friend Shea. She watches everything. But I will get her….eventually.

I'll be seeing you soon.

J

"That little…."

"HARRIET!" I stop her. "No need for that language. I know what he did to Jemma is terrible but please, don't lower yourself to his level, it will throw everything into a panic." I calm her slightly.

There is a knock at the door and we all jump! Three loud, sturdy knocks.

Picture if you will, three women. Two older, one younger, and NO ONE dares to even BREATH let alone move to open the door. This is what it looks like in Mums dining room right this instant, it's almost a comedy sketch!

I finally take a deep breath and check the living room window.

"All clear," I say, "It's Derek."

"Quick, hide the folder!" Harriet cries.

"Uhm….Why?" Mum dares to ask.

"He doesn't know about it, I found it in her room before the police arrived and I hid it from them, I didn't want anyone thinking she was insane, least of all her own father!" Harriet replies defensively.

WHAT!! Why hasn't she told Derek! They never keep secrets from each other! Something isn't right about any of this, but I will find out!

"OK. Mum, hide the papers and the folder for now. We will discuss all this later," I say, looking at Harriet out of the corner of my eye. "Harriet. Hello??" I say, waving my hands in front of her eyes.

"Sorry, yes dear?" She replies, dazed and a little confused.

"Be yourself!" I say, giving her a bright smile, which is the reciprocated.

"Oh, I can do that dear!" She says back.

I do hope so, I think to myself. I'm not sure how Harriet has hidden this from Derek! I'm also not sure how *long* she can hide it. I'm starting to worry about her. *Mental note: break it to Mum that we can't get Harriet too involved. I'm not sure she can handle it alone. Either that or explain all to Derek….Talk to Mum!*

I open the door to a tired looking Derek. He seems to have aged a lot since I saw him after Jemma came back, he seems to have lost a lot of weight too. This must be taking its toll on him. I must admit, he didn't look too good at Jemma's funeral either, but that is to be expected.

"Derek! What a lovely surprise! Come in, sorry it took so long to answer the door; I spilt my drink at the same time!" I say, maybe too cheerfully.

"How much have you had?" He says, laughing and eyeing the half empty bottle on the table. "Not enough, I'd say," he continues, still chuckling to himself.

"Derek, what ARE you doing here?" asks Harriet looking surprised to see him. I let out a silent sigh.

"Looking for you, my angel," he replies sweetly, holding out his hand to her. "I've got fish, chips, and mushy peas for tea."

"Oh you do spoil me!" she replies, taking his outstretched hand.

"Have a lovely evening both of you!" Mum chimes in. "I will call round tomorrow Harriet, we'll have lunch."

"That would be wonderful Lenora; it's just what she needs, thank you," Derek says, "Good evening to you both."

When they were on their way down the street, I close and double lock the door again. What is wrong with me? I call out to Mum and explain how I think it is getting too much for Harriet, she shouldn't be jumping at every noise, and neither should we. Thankfully, Mum agrees.

"Chinese?" Mum asks, surprisingly.

"Why not, my treat!" I say as I grab the phone to place an order.

"Thirty minutes" says Tai, Lins' daughter.

"Fantastic! Thank you Tai!" I reply.

I start to set the table while Mum goes for a quick shower, although it may be a long shower. I saw the tears when Derek came for Harriet, she misses Dad, come on! Who wouldn't! My Dad was amazing. I'm biased I know but he really was.

Jermaine Hopewell was always happy, always laughing and nearly always crying with laughter. He was my hero and I miss him too. He would know what to do with all this. He was a cop after all! Did I forget to mention that?! Whoops!

Chapter 8

Dad had been a police officer for 30 years before he was shot by an overzealous drug addict who a discarded gun and fired at my dad who was working the night shift. They caught the woman, in fact, she handed herself in. She got sent to prison but it won't bring him back. I miss him so much. I can hear the shower switch off. Dammit, I haven't finished setting the table! I must have got lost in thought.

DING DONG

Mmm that will be Lin with the food. I double check before answering. Just as I thought.

"Ah Shea! Twice in one week!" he says cheerfully.

"I can never resist good food!" I smile back, handing over the money but giving more than the cost, it's an added tip for a great service and a great family.

"Thank you Shea. Say hi to your Mum for me!" he says as he turns to leave, waving as he goes.

"I will!" I say, waving back and closing the door.

I go back to the dining room where Mum is stood in Dads' old dressing gown. It swamps her but it brings her comfort and that makes me smile.

"Shall we eat?" I say, with a hint of tears, but ones I'm not willing to let fall in front of Mum. She doesn't need my emotions too.

"Oh definitely! Before it gets cold," she manages.

We settle down to eat, talking about how dad would always steal the prawn crackers without anyone noticing, how he always drank the sweet and sour sauce instead of dipping the chicken balls into it and how he always looked at us like he was the proudest man alive. I remember telling my parents that I wanted to go to Law school. Mum started cry and Dad said he was so proud. They saved up so much to pay for it. They even remortgaged the house. I paid them back as soon as I got my first big pay check. I think I still owe Mum about £10,000. I'll pay her back as soon as I get my next big pay, which should be after my next case.

Mum and I talk until around 10:30pm, then we head off to bed. It's been a long day and I can see how tired Mum is, even if she says otherwise. I have also noticed how pale she has been recently. I make a mental note to ask about her health tomorrow.

For some unknown reason, I can't seem to drop off to sleep straight away, so I just lay there staring at the ceiling. Is that a spider? I squint my eyes in the dark. Nope, not helping! I switch the lamp on to look, definitely not a spider, phew! Turning the lamp back off, I settle back down to try and sleep, but something is still stopping me from sleeping! I just can't put my finger on it. Sitting back up, I pull my laptop out and start searching for clues surrounding Jacks case. I find some news articles from when he abducted the girl, reports from when he skipped the country on the day of his trial and social media reports of possible sightings around the world. If social media is to be believed, he had been in countries that have no extradition laws like China, Egypt and Bahrain. No doubt the police looked into the sightings but without extradition, there isn't much they can do even if they did find him. I spend another hour trailing the internet for clues but to no avail, so I shut my laptop down and attempt to sleep. I keep thinking about Mum, if Jack really is hunting for revenge, and he's already got to Jemma, that means he's looking for me, which means he could hurt Mum to get to me! That's it! Mum will have to come back to London with me. It's the only way I can keep her safe. I wish I could have kept Jemma safe. I feel so guilty for not keeping in close contact with her, or even telling her about my dreams. If I had, she would probably still be alive now, so would Sierra. I'm responsible for two deaths and I can't fix it! As hard as it is, I lay down and force myself to sleep. It's difficult, but I slowly drop off, landing directly into the same wooded area I land night after night, although something is different tonight.

"Shea," someone whisper, "Come over here, quickly."

"Where are you?! I reply, "WHO ARE YOU?"

"Follow my voice, everything will be fine," the voice whispers.

"I don't even know who you are, why should I trust you?" I question.

"You don't really have a choice, do you?" the voice says jokingly.

I think it over; I guess he has a point. I slowly make my way towards the sound, slowly picking my way across the wet, tall grass.

"Shea! Run!"

I hear Jemma's voice for the first time in my dreams.

"RUN SHEA!" Jemma screams

I start running, faster and faster, turning back quickly to see who is behind me. I see the dark eyes, almost burning through my soul. Dark, angry eyes, the anger on his face almost freezes my movement, and my blood, then I remember what happened to Jemma, I turn so quick to run that I don't notice the person in front of me, I smack straight into, what feels like, a brick wall.

That's when I wake up! I quickly write everything down before I forget. That reminds me, search 'can people be killed in their dreams and die in real life', I can't see it being true, but Jemma forced me to watch Nightmare on Elm Street so many times, that I'm starting to think it might be. I really think I'm starting to lose my mind. I check the time, 4:40am. I need some juice.

As I creep, quietly down the hallway towards the stairs I can hear Mum trying to cry quietly. She must have thought I was sleeping. I gently knock on the door.

"Mum?" I ask.

Sniff

"Yes dear, come in, no need to knock," she replies.

"What's wrong Mum?" I ask, slowly opening the door.

"Oh it's just me being an emotional wreck," she says, slipping something under the blanket.

"What are you hiding there, Mum, a secret love letter?" I tease, with a smile. Mum knows I would always support her if she did find another companion.

She looks at me with a serious face and pats the edge of the bed beside her.

"You better sit down darling," she says solemnly.

I sit down expecting her to tell me she has needs as a woman and how she has been seeing someone new since

Dad. I would be happy for her as long as she is happy, but the look in her eyes tells me it's more serious. I'm starting to worry.

"What is it Mum?" I ask.

"Read this love," she says as she passes me the paper from under the blanket.

I open it up and see the words 'BLOOD TEST AND MAMMOGRAM RESULTS'

I quickly read through the letter, practically skimming it for the results.

My Mum has Stage 3 breast cancer.

I look at her with tears in my eyes. I don't know what to say and she understands that. She pulls me in for a hug and we both have a cry together. We will get through this together. We will survive everything life throws at us. We are Hopewells' after all!

We sit for another hour, not really speaking, but just processing things together. I don't think I can even speak without breaking down fully. I was ready to tease her about meeting someone new and all the while she was dealing with this all alone. If the ground could open up right now, I would gratefully jump right in and let it swallow me whole.

After saying goodnight to Mum, I go down to the kitchen to get a drink. I take some time to think about what I had just found out. I need to look into treatment for her, we can beat this. This just solidifies my decision from earlier. She will come back to London with me; I will look into private care for her. She deserves it, but right now, I need to sleep.

When I wake up I realise that I haven't woken up in a sweat. I've woken up very calm and somehow a little more ready to face what awaits me today. Oh! I smell breakfast! Bacon, eggs, and fried bread. My stomach growls at me. I make my way down to the dining room and I'm stunned by what I see. Harriet, Derek, Lana and Louis are all seated around the table while Mum places a plate of bacon in the centre, breakfast buffet style!

"It's nice to see everyone!" I say with a bright smile. "Mum, if I had known you were going to invite guests, I would have made more of an effort!" gesturing at my faded jeans and purple tank top.

"Don't be daft love," Lana laughed, "You look great!"

I smile back at her but I'm still wondering why everyone is here.

Mum approaches me at the kitchen sink. She looks a little apprehensive.

"I'm going to tell everyone about the cancer." she says, trying to show a brave face, but I can see the tears.

"Are you sure Mum?" I ask, gently touching her arm. "I only found out last night."

She gives a stern nod.

"Yes darling, I'm sure. If I haven't got my husband by my side then I am sure as hell going to need my daughter and my friends through this," she says with a small smile and a wink, something her and Dad always did to me.

My heart breaks for her, but I will always be here.

"So Len, what's the deal with breakfast? Don't get me wrong I do love a good brekkie but?" Derek asks, always the first to pick up on something being out of the ordinary.

Derek had always called Mum, Len. He said he full name was a mouthful, but in a good way.

"I asked you all here for a reason. You are all my closest and dearest friends," Mum starts. She takes a deep breath before continuing.

"I have stage 3 breast cancer," she finishes, trying hard not to cry. Harriet is in floods of tears, so I quickly embrace her in a deep hug.

"I will be taking Mum to London for treatment and to look after her when I go back next week," I announce.

Mum looks shocked and, for some reason, upset or sad, I can't tell which.

"Shea, darling, I can't leave this house, no matter what, it's the only place I feel close to your Dad," she says sadly.

"If you do have to go back, we can all take turns to look out for her, we will all make sure she gets to appointments and that she eats well and we will all be there for her," Louis says.

I know they mean well but, well, she's my Mum, surely it should be up to me to look after her. I steal a glance at Mum, she looks so comfortable amongst everyone, and they all paw over her, making sure she is alright. They have always done it. More so since Dad was killed, but they have always been there for us. Mum catches me looking at her and gives me a wink with a wide smile. She's happy here, who am I to disturb that? I smile back and watch how she takes everything in her stride and continues with the breakfast shenanigans, topping up everyone's coffee or tea like a waitress.

After breakfast, everyone gradually leaves, kissing us both on the cheek as they go. I love how Mums friends have dealt with the news, almost like a family does. Perhaps that's how they see us, another branch of the family tree. It's nice to have acceptance and to accept others no matter the situation. I close the door after Derek and Harriet leave, hand in hand. I turn back to Mum and see how exhausted she looks and she's only cooked breakfast!

"Do you want you go and lay down Mum?" I ask, "I'll sort the dishes out."

"Don't be daft Shea!" she says, almost mimicking Lana. "I'll be as right as rain in a minute or two, just need to take my tablets and I'll be set for the day."

"If you're sure," I say, "Do you think you would be up for a walk later?"

"I'd love that dear, we could stop at Jemma and Dads' grave to lay some flowers," she says thoughtfully.

Mum goes off to take her medication whilst I load the dishwasher. Wait! Did I see something in the garden? I'm positive I saw something or someone. Maybe not!

Crash!

"Shea!" Mum shouts.

Chapter 9

'Dearest Shea,

FOUND YOU!

I wish I could say I was sorry about the other girl near Tesco but you have to admit, she did look like you!

Have I got your attention now? I hope so. Maybe you will be the one who will listen to me. Jemma didn't and look what I had to do to her, not that I regret it.

We will meet again soon

J.'

I read the note over and over whilst Mum phones the police. How am I going to explain any of this to them without sounding like a complete crazy woman?

When the police arrive, I attempt to explain the whole situation while they stare at me with a blank expression. They obviously don't believe a single word I'm saying so I stop. They blink in unison with each other, like a cartoon. PC

Booth takes a deep breath, almost like it is a task for his tall, slender frame.

"Just to clarify, you believe this note to be from a Jack Woodwin, who abducted a child just over 2 years ago and skipped the country on his trial date?" he asks.

"As crazy as it sounds, yes," I reply, with as much sturdiness as my voice can manage right now.

WPC Ryles just gives me a cold stare that makes my soul wish it could skip the universe.

"You do realise how odd this sounds, especially coming from a lawyer? We've run a check on the name and there's nothing showing up about him being back in the country," she shares, with a hint of annoyance.

"Yes I do realise that, and it's obvious there won't be any details as he is on false documents," I remind her, after explaining this, at least 4 times already.

She walks away, radio in hand. PC Booth mutes his radio which proves she is radioing about me. He then asks me to sit down and try to remember anything odd about the moment leading up to the brick coming through Mums bedroom window. I talk him through everything and even give him Louis and Lana and Derek and Harriets' numbers to clarify that they were here too. As WPC Ryles returns from her impromptu tour of Dads roses and lavender plants in the garden, she informs her colleague that a senior member of the force will be taking over. They will contact in due course.

'Yes Shea, they think you really are bat do-do crazy! Brilliant!' I say to myself while guiding them to the front door.

"Thanks for coming" I say, as cheerfully as I can.

They smile as I close the door behind them.

'Thanks for nothing' I say to myself.

Mum still looks shaken up so I quickly call Lana and Harriet to ask if they could come and keep Mum company whilst I nit to the shop for some essentials, namely wine and chocolate. As fast as I'd called, they arrived at the door carrying board games and playing cards. I'm so glad Mum has such great friends like these. They sit with Mum, and I make some tea for them, explaining how and why Mum is a bit shaky. We say its kids accidentally throwing rocks and it works. The police think I'm off my rocker but I don't want Lana thinking that too! Judging by the look on Harriets' face she knows I'm bending the truth, but she says nothing.

I take a short walk to the local corner shop, this way I don't have to venture too far from Mum. I worry about her. Even before all this happened. As I near the shop, I see Liam again. It suddenly occurs to me that I hadn't seen him since Jemma's funeral, not even around town.

"Liam?" I call out.

"Hey Shea!" he replies, "How have you been?"

"Up and down if I'm honest," I reply, "Where are you living now? I haven't seen you since the funeral," I ask.

"Oh I don't live in Leeds anymore," he replies, "I'm here on holiday mainly and looking after Mum."

"I didn't realise," I reply back, "How is your Mum these days?"

"She's comfortable, shall we say," he says. "She hasn't had it easy recently, she was mugged a few weeks back, broke her arm and her hip when he pulled her over."

"Did they catch him?" I ask, hopefully.

"In the end yeah, he'd spent all the cash but Mum was quick enough to cancel her cards," he says with a smile.

"Phew!" I sigh out loud.

"When are you leaving?" we both say in unison.

This follows promptly by hysterical laughter.

"I'm going back to London next week," I say.

"That's a shame. I'm heading back to the USA in a few hours. It would have been nice to catch up properly." He says. "Pass me your email address and we can stay in contact."

I write down all my contact details and tell him to give his Mum a hug from me. I turn and head into the shop. I manage to grab a nice bottle of wine and some really nice, fancy chocolates. But as I walk back towards Mums' I can feel someone following me. I duck into the chemist and watch as a sneaky Yvette walks straight past.

Why is she following me? I think to myself. She never really wanted to know me and Jemma at school, so why is she so interested in me now? She probably wants some gossip about the night the police were in Mums' living room. It's baffling, she never showed any interest before.

I leave the chemist and take a different route home. Just in case she is waiting somewhere else.

After getting back to Mums, I notice Harriet and Lana have taken her out, probably for a walk.

I find a note stuck to the fridge with the magnet picture of my graduation, seems so long ago now.

Shea,

We've taken Len to visit your Dad.

She wants to tell him.

We will keep her safe.

Love and hugs.

L and H

X

Those two are so close to Mum, they remind me of myself and Jemma....and Sabrina Wellbury. Sabrina was like our third part. We didn't know her long, maybe 3 years or less. She joined our secondary school in Year 9. We all just got along, so well. We were always laughing, meeting up at weekends and never in trouble. We never really met Sabrinas' family. She was really private about that. We never met up near her house; in fact, I don't think we even knew which house was hers until that day. The day we lost our third.

Chapter 10

Sabrina was a quiet girl when she was alone, but when we were altogether, she was totally different, she was like the sun. She never really spoke about her home life; we never knew if she had brothers or sisters, we didn't even know her parents, we never saw them.

Until the day she was found hanged at home.

That's when we found out why she never spoke about her family. Her stepdad was always drunk, he would beat her Mum so badly, and she would be unconscious for hours, long enough for him to sexually assault Sabrina without her Mum knowing. It had been going on for 6 years. She put on a smile for the outside world but inside she was screaming for help and couldn't tell anyone.

When the police released the details, our school held an assembly and encouraged us all to 'Speak Out'. As students, we were offered counselling as a way of helping us deal with what had happened. Some students talked to counsellors but Jemma and I didn't. We vowed to never speak of it again; we never forgot her or what happened to her. Her stepdad was sentenced to 8 years in prison and her Mum committed suicide on the day of the sentencing. Just seeing Mum, Harriet and Lana together made me cry inside because, as Sabrinas' friends, we had failed to protect her and we vowed to never let anyone down again. That's when we decided on our career path. We did it for Sabrina. I took advantage of the empty house to read through some more of Jemmas diary.

'25th August 2017 – Jemma

Today has been strange. Went out shopping with Shea this morning. Took a stroll around Oxford Street. Brought a few nice outfits, some for work, loads for play! I wish Shea would come with me, but she doesn't like it.

I swear someone was following us, I felt like someone was watching us all day. I didn't mention it to Shea; she would probably say I'm still hung-over from last night. I didn't sleep well last night. He was there again, chasing us. I hid so well again, but he keeps getting closer to Shea. I don't want to

tell her about my dreams. She probably won't believe me anyway.'

'Oh Jemma,' I think to myself, trying not to cry. 'I would have believed you; I was dreaming the same thing.'

We used to tell each other everything, but after we were given that case, things just changed. Jemma wasn't the same. I wasn't the same. That case would have been another major case under our belts, we could have made progress up the chain and have a chance at bigger cases.

After that case went south, which was faster than birds in winter, we weren't set any cases together. That's when Jemmas' drinking got worse. She mentioned once, that she struggled to work alone. That she couldn't handle the work load alone. I offered to give her a hand with case notes but she kept saying no. What more could I do? I was working 3 cases to her one major case.

I quickly grab my diary to compare it to Jemmas'.

'25th August 2017 – Shea

I managed to get Jemma to come shopping with me this morning. We spent some time looking around Oxford Street. I managed to buy a few things, a couple of new suits for work and something for Mum's birthday.

Jemma kept looking back almost like she wanted to run. Run like I have been doing in my dreams. Running through the long, wet grass. Someone chasing me, I can't tell Jemma though, she will probably just tell me I'm working too hard.'

Practically the same entry. I wish we hadn't have drifted apart after that case. I tried so hard to get things back to how they were before, but I think we had just grown up at different rates. Wanted different things from our lives. To go in different directions. Everything changed for us as we grew up. We realised we weren't teenagers anymore. I realised it was only me who wanted this career after all. Jemma just wanted the money. She didn't want to work for the money, just wanted to cash the cheque, so to speak.

Thinking back to the cases we worked on, I was always doing the work. She would speak up on the odd occasion, but nothing fundamental that would aid the case. Why didn't I notice it before? Or did I just not want to admit what I was seeing? I didn't want to admit to myself that I was losing my best friend. That no matter how much I pushed her to be a part of this career, she really didn't want it as much as I did.

Chapter 11

I can hear the all chatting and giggling before they come through the door. At least Mum is smiling now, thanks to her friends. A tear comes to my eye. I miss my friend. My best friend. I miss Jemma. I close everything up and slide it away before they crash through the kitchen door.

"There you all are!" I say cheekily, "I was about to send out the search party!"

"Oh Shea, sorry we went without you," Mum replies, "I went to see your Dad, I had to tell him about the cancer."

"I should have been with you. I'm sorry you had to do that alone Mum", I cry into her shoulder as she gives me a tight squeeze.

"We will leave you both to it," Lana and Harriet say together. "You know to call if you need us."

"Thank you both," I say, "For everything." I give a small smile and a slight wave as they leave.

"How are you feeling Mum?" I ask, gently pulling out of her embrace.

"I'm good honey, I feel so much better after talking to you Dad," she smiles. "He's watching over us both."

"He certainly is Mum," I agree. "He's never stopped."

I go to the kitchen to make some tea, pulling out two cups, I notice Dads cup still at the front of the cupboard, dusty and a constant reminder that he is never coming back. I take it out and give it a quick rinse, dry it and put it back in place.

"I love you Dad," I whisper.

I take the tea into Mum, who has drifted off to sleep in Dads chair. I think the trip to the cemetery has brought her closure with Dads death. I lay a blanket softly over her, give her a gentle kiss on the forehead and tiptoe back into the kitchen. I place the folder, diaries, laptop and my notepad on the kitchen table and settle down for some more investigating. I've got to find out what is happening before it gets worse. Could it get any worse?

I turn page after page through Jemma's folder. Sketches show the same face, pieces of paper with dates and sightings.

'*Fountain in town, 1:15pm Saturday 2nd September 17*'

'*Subway Take Away, 11:10am Monday 4th September 17*'

'*Outside local pub, 7:15pm Wednesday 6th September 17*'

List after list of times she had seen him. One listing, Friday 15th September 17, lists him as being at Wire nightclub wearing blue denim jeans, matched with a blue shirt and black shoes.

'*15th September 17 – Jemma.*

He was at the club tonight. I saw him, clear as day. He looked straight at me, smiled too, that creepy smile that chills me to my soul. I told the bouncers he was stalking me.

They just laughed, said I'd had too much to drink and called me a taxi to take me home. Mum weren't happy. Good job I go back to London on Monday.

I remember that weekend. We had come back to visit briefly. Something was freaking Jemma out but I just put it down to work stress. It was Mums birthday on the 15th so we had gone into town for a meal and birthday drinks. Jemma had gone off on her own after a while, saying it was boring just sitting around. I went to follow her but Harriet said to leave her to it and that she was being selfish.

I stayed awake most of the night that night. Worried about Jemma but terrified to sleep because of the dreams. I saw the taxi bring her home; it slowed past Mums to let the bus past. I saw the fear in her eyes but I put it down to a bad time at the club. Why didn't I ask her about it? I feel so guilty.

"Shea love, are you alright?" Mum asks softly.

"Oh Mum, you made me jump! Yeah, I'm fine, just reliving days through Jemma's diary." I say.

"Sorry I made you jump darling." She says, giving my shoulder another quick squeeze. "What have you found out?"

I explain to Mum about the weekend in September and how guilty I feel because I didn't question Jemma's mood. Mum gives me the look Mums give you when you're speaking absolute nonsense.

"There is nothing to feel guilty about. Jemma was a very troubled girl then and judging by all this, we can now see why!" she says, as she gestures the complete mess I've made of the table.

I know she is trying to make me feel better. It's not working but I don't tell her that, I just smile.

I ask Mum if she remembers that weekend. She sits for a few minutes with her eyes shut.

'Great!' I think to myself, 'She's nodded off again!'

"It's so vivid, it's almost like it was yesterday," she says from absolutely nowhere. "We were getting ready to go to that nice little Italian restaurant, the one with the little candles in red vases."

"I know the one. Dad always took you there for your anniversary," I reply with a sweet smile, remembering all the times Dad had pre-booked the table weeks in advance. How he had bought the biggest bunch of red roses from the flower shop just to show how much Mum meant to him.

"Jemma was very agitated and fidgety. She was fiddling with her nails and her hair the whole time whilst Harriet and I tried to straighten your hair!" Mum giggles as if remembering all the fuss that evening. Just to let you know, it never straightened!

"Jemma couldn't sit still for long, she kept looking out the window, then at the time and then back out the window. Harriet snapped at her about it, even going as far as to jokingly ask if she had taken anything." Mum remembers fondly.

"I remember Harriet saying that and then laughing afterwards. Jemma looked so hurt, almost like she wanted to tell her Mum everything, but she was too scared." I say, my mind swimming back to that evening.

The look on Jemma's face, almost crying out for the help that no one was offering, she wanted help but didn't have the confidence to ask for it. I quickly grab my diary and turn to the same date, cross referencing everything. The only differences were that I didn't go to the club. I even wrote about seeing her in the taxi and how scared she looked. I don't know why but I started crying, sobbing hard that I wasn't a good friend, how I let her down when she needed me the most. Mum held me until I was so tired from crying.

She led me up to bed and tucked me in like I was a child again, kissing my forehead and switching off the light as I drifted off to sleep.

'I'm running again, through the wet, slippery grass, towards the thickness of the trees ahead. I've slipped over twice; I can feel the wetness through my jeans. I can still hear the deep, harsh breathing. I stop behind the tallest, widest oak tree and slide down the trunk to the floor. I lay, belly down, on the dirty floor, hoping he runs past my hiding spot. He stops, looks towards where I am silently hiding. I can see his silhouette against the moonlight.

"Shea," comes the whisper, "Crawl towards my voice."

"Who are you?" I whisper back. "How do I know you won't hurt me?"

"I'm here to help you. Nothing more. I promise." Comes the reply.

I'm not entirely convinced, but there is something comforting about the voice to I begin a slow, hopefully silent, crawl towards it.

"Finally, you've made it!" says a stark white skinned man. "It's taken me a while to copy the pattern of your running and to be in the ideal place to bring you to the safest part," he continued.

"Sorry to be blunt," I say, staring at the sheer brightness of his red hair, "Who are you exactly and why are you in my dream?"

"All will be revealed soon," he says, "Right now, you need to listen closely. When you wake, you need to make your way to the place you and Jemma used to hide when your parents called you for tea. There you will find a possible reason for me being here, something more than that folder you already have."

With that he was gone. All around me were the brightest daffodils I had ever seen.'

I wake up slowly this morning, still trying to work out what happened in my dream. I remember my diary is downstairs, so I put my dressing gown on and quietly slip down to get it.

Halfway down I hear voices. I stop on the step before the squeaky one, amazed I even remember which one it is!

"No, she's still sleeping. I will get her to call you when she wakes up," I hear Mum say.

"It's important we speak with your daughter Mrs Hopewell," I hear a sterner voice say.

"I said I will get her to call you when she wakes up!" Mum says with more dominance.

"As you wish, Ma'am," the sterner voice says, buckling under the sheer dominance of Mums voice. She has had the practice having to talk over my Dad in the past. "Please insist she call us right away."

Mum closes the door with a slam, muttering to herself how rude he was.

"Mum?" I say, softly enough that I didn't startle her.

"How long have you been there?" she asks.

"Long enough," I say with a grin, "Who was it?"

"Some jumped up policeman and his lapdog." She says, grinning back at me.

"Mum!" I say, trying not to laugh at her, "Who was he really?"

"Oh, your Dad trained him when he was a rookie cop, now he's a detective, he thinks he is the dogs doo-dahs!" she replies. "Don't know who he thinks he is, coming here and demanding to speak to you that instant! Not under my roof sonny!"

You really have to love my Mum. She knows her right especially under her own roof. She was a cop's wife after all!

"Where is his number and my diary Mum?" I ask.

"Just on the table sweetheart. I hope you don't mind, but I had a quick read through of some of it, why didn't you come to me baby?" She says with a tear in her eye.

"I was too scared to admit I was scared Mum. I hoped it was all a dream." I say trying not to let my voice crack under the immense pressure not to cry on Mums shoulder again. I grab my diary and the number and after giving Mum a hard squeeze, go upstairs to write everything down and get dressed. It seems I'm on a mission today. I really hope I'm not losing my mind. Imagine trying to explain to someone that I am looking for something a man in my dreams told me to find! Crazy, huh!?

I decide to call the number from my mobile on the way to our secret spot, the tallest tree in the wooded area nearby. I dial the number as I walk and wait for an answer.

"DCI Wetherby speaking. How can I help?" Comes the blunt voice.

"Hello, this is Shea Hopewell. I believe you wanted to speak to me urgently?" I reply, stopping myself from barking back at him.

"Ah, Miss Hopewell, thank you for calling. I wanted to ask you about the letter attached to the rock that was thrown through your mother's window yesterday," he says, with a slightly more polite voice now.

"What exactly would you like to know that the officers didn't note down yesterday? They took the note in as evidence; I don't see how I can be of much more help." I ask, harsher than I intended.

"The officers forgot to ask if you knew who could have possibly sent it. It was only signed *J*?" he asks.

"I know exactly who sent it, his name is Jack Woodwin. I will offer some information on him before you ask. He was due in court 2 years ago, charges were kidnap and assault. He fled the day of his court appearance and hasn't been seen since. As a prosecutor in that very case, I believe he fled the country. We've chased paper trails for nearly 2 years, so if you intend to look for him, I wish you the best of luck!" I ended the call.

I head towards the woods, briskly walking towards the tallest, oldest tree here. I look up and take in its majestic appearance. It doesn't look quite as big as it did before, but that probably because I haven't been here in over 20 years!

I look around the base of the tree, memories flooding back like a tsunami of Jemma and I running rings around this tree. I smile to myself as I remember how much fun we had when we were children. I take a deep breath and remember what the strange guy from my dream said to me, that something was here for me to find, but where could it be? If something was left here then, surely, someone would have picked it up by now. *Think Shea, think!* I almost shout at myself. I close my eyes and let my mind take me back to the times we hid from our parents. Where was it? My eyes fly open at the sudden memory! I dig around the bottom of the tree. We used to hide in the opening at the base of the tree. We could both fit inside and no one could find us, we never stayed in there long though, just long enough to hear our parent's threats! I uncover the hole, removing dried grass, sharp brambles and rotting tree roots. There is it! I look inside, there's something there! I reach inside, trying to avoid the sticky and silky spider webs that try to block my way. It feels like a book, a very 'old' book.

'The Power of Moon Magic'

Moon magic? What on Earth?

I open the book to the first page and a picture of me falls to the floor. This is just too spooky now, I'm contemplating going home now and leaving this book here. I'm not sure if I'm ready for this. The next thing to fall from the book is an envelope with my name scribed across the front, in a font I've only ever seen in Shakespearean books. I don't open it right away. I gather the book and the envelope and sit on the dead tree trunk that Jemma and I used to sit on when we were children. I needed to focus on this.

I take a deep breath and gently open the delicate envelope.

'Dear Shea,

If you are reading this, then this book has done its job. You are my best friend and I want to save you from him. I know he is coming for us, I've seen him in my dreams. He is always chasing us, he wants revenge. He won't stop until he has it. I have used this book to manipulate your dreams and used its magic to place a 'saviour' inside them. You will know him when you see him, his name is Zephyr. He will guide you but only through your dreams, don't be afraid to look for him or call out to him.

My dear Shea, I'm sorry for everything, please forgive me.

Eternal love

Jemma xx

As I read the words, I can't help but cry.

"Oh Jemma, there's nothing to forgive," I say out loud. "I wish you could forgive me for being a terrible friend."

I put the book and letter in to my tote bag and prepare to leave. That's when I hear the 'crak'. The sudden snapping of a nearby twig; someone is here, possibly watching my every move. I don't move, I daren't breathe. I turn slowly and catch a glimpse of him in the thicket of trees; he is glaring at me with dark, cold angry eyes. If I need a saviour, I need him now!

I grab my back and just run. I don't even look back. I'm too scared. How did he know where I would be? Has he been following me? If he has, I can't let him catch me out, I have to think and plan ahead, I can't let him get to me, but I have to be able to catch him out. I know these woods well so I know I won't get lost, but he doesn't, this is my chance to lose him and get home before he works his way out.

I take a left and duck down; I crawl, as best as I can, towards the lake at the centre of the woods, hoping someone would be there. Definitely not my day, it's deserted. I duck behind the bird hide and wait for two minutes before changing direction again. I head right, then take a sharp left and emerge on the road. I can't see him but I can hear him.

"You can't hide from me," he puffs. "I will find you!"

"Not today you won't. I'm not ready...yet," I say, quietly.

I make my way towards Mum's but make a split decision to change course to the police station, just to give them an update. You can never give too much information into an investigation.

DCI Wetherby isn't in the office so I am directed to DI Coyle. She is a petite woman with ashen skin and raven black hair, she looks almost deathly, but she is kind and soft spoken. She offers me a seat and a cup of tea. I, then, tell her what happened mere minutes before.

DI Coyle takes pages of notes, from the time, down to the location and description of Jack. She looks a little taken aback, but I take this at face value. Judging by how timid she is, I can only guess that she hasn't been in the job very long, and this might well be her first major case. I warn her that he changes his appearance often, which she noted down too. She was just about to finish when DCI Wetherby bursts into the room.

"What are you doing in here Coyle?" he demands, "This is my investigation!"

"I was just taking some notes sir," she replies quietly. "I did try to contact you before the interview."

"Well you obviously didn't try hard enough!" he raises his voice some more, more than necessary. "Get out!"

She dips her head apologetically and leaves the room. I feel a pang of sympathy and anger for her. This 'man' was not the police officer my father would have taught him to be. Maybe seniority had gone to his head!

He looks at me dead in the eyes, almost trying to psychoanalyze me without talking to me. After 3 minutes, he opens his hands in a defeated manner and says, "Are you going to tell me or do I have to attempt mind reading?"

"Read your colleagues notes and you won't have to attempt anything except some gratitude!" I say bluntly.

He sat up straighter.

"You DO NOT speak to me like that. I am your superior, no one is above the law!" he says, slamming his palms on the table and if to scare me.

"You don't frighten me DCI Wetherby," I say calmly. "I have dealt with far more threatening people that you throughout my career."

I stand ready to leave. He clears his throat.

"Something to say, DCI?" I prompt.

"You are very much like your father," he says almost like a scorned child.

"Well, I know my Dad would NEVER have taught you to speak to people the way you do," I say. "Good day."

I close the door calmly behind me, taking a deep breath. I spot DI Coyle sitting in the waiting area. I smile to her as I walk.

"Does he always speak like that? Please don't cover for him," I ask politely.

"When he's worked up, yes. More so on big cases like yours. There isn't much I can do though, I'm only six months into the job." She replies quietly, almost terrified he will hear her confession.

"There is something you can do. Stand up to him. He is only human, just like you and I." I say with a gentle squeeze of her shoulder. "Take care."

I leave the police station, cautiously looking for signs of Jack. When I am confident he hasn't tracked me here, I start to walk back to Mums. I hold my bag just a little bit tighter walking through town. I scan every face, settling my mind that he isn't around. Something stands out though. Didn't Jemma say...? No it can't be. Could it? I chance calling out to him. What harm could it do? If it's not him, I can claim I have tourettes!

"ZEPHYR?" I shout.

A few people turn their heads to look at me. I smile sweetly at them, I'm not about to explain myself. Yes, I look crazy but I don't care. Jemma specifically said I could only see him in my dreams, so why am I, now, looking straight at him, and right across the high street.

"Oh darn," he says, walking towards me. "You weren't supposed to see me!"

"Kind of hard not to," I gesture to his hair and complexion, "You don't exactly blend in," I laugh.

We walk and talk, so we aren't sitting ducks if Jack did decide to make an appearance.

"Jemma wrote that you could only been reached through my dreams. How are you here?" I ask, inquisitively.

"It's hard to explain, but I'll try," he says, thinking what to say next. "First we have to find somewhere undercover, something isn't quite right here." he finishes, looking around nervously.

We duck inside a dimly lit restaurant and ask for a table for two away from the window. Once seated, I order a cold drink, Zephyr politely declines. I wonder if he can even drink or eat. I call Mum whilst waiting for my drink, just to let her know I'm ok and not to worry. Lana is at Mums again. Bridge night apparently! Who knew?! My mind at ease with Mum's safety, I turn back to Zephyr. I watch him survey his surroundings, taking mental notes of the people he can see. He was really easy on the eye, but he had an otherworldly look about him, I mean he stood out from everyone else but in a good way. Women would look in his direction and take a second glance to verify what they saw the first time. His bright red hair was silky smooth and his complexion, although pale, was perfect. His eyes stood out the most; they were the darkest brown with the tiniest pupils, almost like a pinprick of black.

"So Zephyr," I start, "Explain how you seemed to escape my dreams!"

"I'll explain but you have to promise not to interrupt." He says, calmly.

I promise and sit ready to listen, this should be interesting, and hopefully a breath of fresh air compared to everything else that is happening.

"Are you sitting comfortably? Then I'll begin." He says with a smile.

Ha! He sounds like my Dad at bedtime!

Chapter 12

"Let me get this straight," I say, when he has explained. "Jemma thought she had only summoned you to save me via my dreams, but she really conjured you to do both?"

"That's the quickest way of saying it, yes." He replies, eyes still scanning the area. "I can walk through both worlds just as easily as you can walk through doors."

I think about this for a minute. So many questions but where to start?

"Can you just 'appear'? Like magic?" I ask, then realising how daft I sound.

"No, I can only appear if I sense you are in danger, like today," he says, this time his eyes are on me. "He was near you and I could feel your fear. I just walked towards the sense and there you were."

"But I wasn't scared here, it was in the woods. It was like he followed me there." I say, reliving the whole thing in my head. The icy stare he gave me, as if he could see into my soul.

"I know, hence why I shifted the layout of the woods slightly, just enough for him to go round in circles and long enough for you to escape," he says with a Cheshire cat smile. "He's probably found his way out by now."

"You can do that?" I ask, surprised.

"I can only shift it by a small margin, then it shifts back after a few minutes, fifteen at the most," he says, as if this is all normal.

"So if you can only get here via my fear, how do you get back? Do I have to go to sleep or?" I ask, shrugging my shoulder.

"Ha Ha," he laughs. "No, I just walk down that alley over there and then I'm gone. No one even notices that I don't re-emerge," he says, still acting as if this is normality.

I roll my eyes. I think it is time to head back to Mums. I need some normality after today.

I watch Zephyr walk down the alleyway with no one paying him any attention. Then that's it! He's gone! Like he was never here.

I take the main road back to Mums that way is anything did happen; there would be plenty of witnesses. As I'm walking, I start going over everything in my head. Making mental notes as I go. Research everything to do with Moon Magic, careful to ignore craziness on forums. Continue reading through Jenna's folder, hopefully there is something in there about Zephyr. So many things to do including my case notes for next month's trial. I wish I could take more time off. Maybe if I call Tandy tomorrow and request another week. I've never taken time off before so surely I'm owed some time. Mental notes made, I speed up walking, and I make it home just in time to see Lana leaving.

"Good game you two?" I ask cheerfully.

"She beat me three times!" Lana says, holding up three fingers.

"You had bad hands!" Mum laughed. "It was still fun all the same!"

"Good night!" we all say together, and then laugh about it. We watch her walk to her house then close and lock the door.

"Did you have a good day dear?" Mum asks, "Have you eaten all day?"

For a second I just stood there, deep in thought.

"Shea?" Mum says, as she waves her hand across my eyes, "The light is on but you seem to have left the building."

"Huh?" I say, finally. "Sorry Mum, I was miles away, what did you say?"

"I hope it was somewhere nice!" She says with a smile. "I asked if you had eaten yet."

"Oh, erm, not that I can remember," I reply, "So much has happened today so I might just take a long bath and then make some pasta afterwards, if that's ok?"

"Of course darling," She says. "Lana and I ate earlier. I'll run you a bath."

Once Mum was in the bathroom, I pulled the book from my bag. I admired the binding of it. It had clearly been cared for, the leather cover was in perfect condition although a little dusty. I turned to the first page, sweeping my hand over the page lightly. With the picture and Jemmas' letter safely in my bag, I began to read:

'What you read in this book must only be used in dire circumstances. If you do not fully understand what it is you are attempting, seek expert advice.

The circumstances of using magic without proper training can be devastating! Especially Moon Magic. Remember! You could change the course of one's' life should you get this wrong.

It is not unknown for deaths to occur.'

'Wow' I think, 'That last line is a bit strong!'

I close the book when I hear the bathroom door open, thank goodness for the squeak! I am glad Mum didn't oil it! I don't think I can explain this to her yet. I don't even understand it myself.

"Your bath is ready dear," Mum says, drying her hands on her trousers.

"Thanks Mum, I laugh, as I throw her a tea towel.

She catches it with ease. I open the fridge to pour a glass of orange juice just as the doorbell chimes. We both freeze and look at each other.

"You expecting anyone Mum?" I ask cautiously.

"No dear. You?" She replies.

"No, no one from work actually knows the address I'm staying at," I say, making my way to the door. I slide the chain on for added security. "Who is it?"

"DCI Wetherby, Miss Hopewell. May I come in?" replies the voice.

"Please hold you ID up to the peephole," I say.

"Certainly," he replies, holding his badge and warrant card up for me to see.

I open the door slightly, enough to see him but not enough for him to try to barge in.

"Good evening Miss Hopewell, Mrs Hopewell," he says, glancing over my shoulder. "May I come in?"

"I don't know if I should let you after the way you spoke today." I say, confidently. I will not allow a man to try to control me.

"I would appreciate it greatly. I do apologise for my attitude and unprofessionalism earlier," he directs the last part towards Mum.

"Oh let the poor boy in Shea! He is a police officer after all," She says, sarcastically.

"I wouldn't care if he was the King of England, Mum. I don't care for his treatment of women!" I reply, walking back to the open fridge.

I knew he wasn't happy with what I had said, but Dad taught me to speak my mind and that is what I will do.

I sit at the table whilst Mum makes him a cup of tea. I keep my head held high, also something dad taught me to do, it shows I'm not a pushover, he taught me that when I was seven and I've always remembered it. DCI Wetherby makes small talk with Mum for a while, about the weather and how he is looking forward to some 'well needed time off', if I was his boss, I'd make him work twice as hard just to earn a day off!

"Oh Shea, I nearly forgot, I must call Harriet and arrange lunch for tomorrow." Mum says, getting up from the table, "Excuse me Detective."

He smiles as she darts up the stairs. Then he turns to me.

"How can I help you Detective?" I begin, "I'm sure you don't normally conduct house calls at 7:30pm?"

"I didn't want to mention anything in front of your mother; I'm not sure how much she knows about today." He says in a somewhat different attitude from earlier.

"She doesn't know anything, yet," daring him to say something to her.

"I won't say anything as it isn't my place to do so," he begins, "I would like to apologise for my behaviour earlier. I have no excuse and I'm sure you wouldn't believe one if I did. I have also apologised to DI Coyle."

"Apology accepted, now, was there anything else?" I ask.

"Yes actually. If you don't mind, I'd like to take a walk to the area in which you saw Jack today, could we meet tomorrow morning, say, 9:30am by the fountain?" he finishes.

I think for a moment, maybe a moment longer than I needed to, just to prove who was in charge here. It seems he is now keen to find out exactly what is happening. Still, I will take all at face value.

"Sure, I'll see you then."

I show DCI Wetherby to the door and carefully lock it again behind him. I grab my bag and head for the stairs. I had nearly forgotten about my bath.

That's when I notice the slip of paper sticking through the letterbox, I'm positive it wasn't there when I closed the door.

I set my bag down and take the paper in my hands. Instantly recognising the handwriting, I grab my phone and hit redial.

"Get here now!" I shout down the phone.

"Shea?" Mum says from the stairs, "What is it?"

"Go upstairs Mum, please, and lock your bedroom door," I say to her.

She does as I ask, but reluctantly. I'm scared for her safety now.

Chapter 13

I open the door at the first knock and pull him inside, scanning the street before closing the door.

"What's happened Shea?" DCI Wetherby asks.

"I found this stuck through the door just after you left," I say, showing him the paper.

He takes some gloves from his pocket and carefully takes the paper to the kitchen. He unfolds it to reveal a letter made up of cut out letters.

"Poison pen letter," he says after he had laid it out flat. "I'll call forensics; they might be able to get something. Did anyone else besides you touch it?"

"No, I sent Mum upstairs. She has stage 3 breast cancer. I don't want to worry her." I reply, knowing I will have to tell her something.

I call Harriet; asking her to come and get Mum and could she stay there tonight. Harriet comes almost instantly with Derek in tow. I quickly explain as much as I can about what's happened without upsetting anyone too much, but Harriet looks worried. I can't blame her. I'm terrified myself.

As Mum leaves for Harriet's, she looks back and smiles. She knows I'm doing this for her safety. I just wish I didn't have to do this at all. Jemma should still be here. I shouldn't be chasing after answers as to why Jack waited two years to put this all into action, but here I am, playing detective. Wait a minute! I could possibly have a detective or two at my current disposal. Could I trust them enough to let them help? I don't want them to take over, just help.

"DCI Wetherby? DI Coyle? Would it be possible to have a quiet word?" I ask, noticing how quickly his partner had arrived after his phone call.

"Of course," they both say, looking at each other with obvious question.

I lead them to the kitchen table and gesture for them to take a seat. Once seated, I pull out Jemmas folder; their eyes grow wide with amazement. I can see the questions forming.

"Now," I say, "Before I begin to let you both in on this, you have to promise to help ONLY, not try and take over. This is MY investigation." I say the last sentence whilst looking directly at DCI Wetherby, mimicking his words from earlier in the day.

They share a glance, but not a single word. They both nod in agreement. Well, that was easier than I expected, especially from DCI Wetherby! I, briskly, nod once, and then pull out the sketch from Jemma's folder. The sketch of Jack. I know this is all going to sound completely crazy to two cops who, quite possibly think I'm already a complete nutcase, but it's worth it. They have additional resources I can't access, like mobile phone records, and CCTV to name a few.

DI Coyle takes the sketch in her hands, which start to visibly shake. She pulls it closer to her face, turning it slightly towards the light. I know Jemma wasn't the best at drawing but she tried her best.

"Do you happen to have a picture from before he changed his look?" She asks, nervously.

"I can access my case notes from then on my laptop. I'm sure there was a picture of him there" I reply, tapping a few keys before a picture emerges on the screen.

I turn the laptop around, providing access for DI Coyle.

DI Coyle gasps.

We both look at her with questioning eyes. She struggles back to her seat; I grab her elbow just before she sinks her head in her hands and silently cries.

"Coyle? What is it?" DCI Wetherby asks, softly.

This is as attentive as I have ever seen him and it shows him in a new light, maybe it is his job that affects his attitude.

"Do you know him?" he presses, whilst resting his hand on her shoulder.

She nods her head hard.

"How well?" he asks, slightly sterner this time, which worries me.

She takes a deep breath, holds her head up. Her eyes are red and swollen; the ashen face now a shade of crimson.

"Take a look for yourself," she says, pointing at the screen. "That's Elijah," she says looking me in the eyes. "He's my husband."

I take a step back from them both and sink into the depths of my own mind. In the distance, I can hear DCI Wetherby cursing. He sounds angry but why? I slowly resurface, and it takes me a couple of breaths to realise she's telling the truth. DCI Wetherby is still cursing to high heavens. He must be friends with this man. So he didn't skip the country after all. He was here the whole time, probably watching our every move, watching our career, laughing the whole time Jemma's career went down the drain. I can vaguely hear DCI Wetherby talking to her.

"Skye." He says. "How could you not know anything about his past? Didn't you think to check?"

"Oh Kyron, it's so hard to explain," she says. "It was a really fast proposal and marriage. He told me he had never loved anyone like he loved me. He helped me study to get where I am, he was there for me when my parents died. He was so supportive of everything I did. Two years of perfection."

This is the first time I've heard them speak to each other with such compassion and informality. It's very rare for officers to use their first names whilst on duty. She turns to see me staring blankly out of the kitchen window. I have no idea how I got here, but here I stand, staring at my own reflection.

"I'm so sorry," I vaguely hear her say. I turn slowly, almost too scared to move let alone speak. I don't trust my own voice but I test it out.

"You...weren't to know," I manage, somehow. "No-one knew where he went. The trail went cold in the same week he went missing but we all kept looking. He could have just taken the sentencing and he would have been out by now." I ended, nearly out of breath.

Skye breaks down again.

"He told me he had just come out of a messy marriage and divorce. He had divorce papers and everything," she sobbed. "How did I become a detective and not sniff out that they were possible fakes!"

I start to wonder how she could just believe everything I'm saying without even a hint of defence for him. I don't want to hint at anything in front of Kyron so I ask for a few minutes alone with Skye. Just to talk.

"Skye?" I ask, softly. "Why do you instantly believe he's guilty?"

She sighed as if a weight had been lifted from her shoulders, a weight she had been carrying for a lifetime.

"I had some doubts when we first started dating," she says. "He wanted to get married after six months, said he had never felt like this before and he didn't want it to end."

She paused to gain her composure some more before continuing with the barrage of events that happened after.

"I spoke to my parents about him and the marriage, Mum was very suspicious to start with but Dad, all he wanted was a decent man who would look after his daughter well." She explains.

Before she can continue, a nearby clearing of a throat stops her.

"Sorry to disturb you both," says a boyish looking officer, his freckles showing up more on his face the redder it becomes. "I was wondering if you had seen DCI Wetherby, I can't seem to locate him."

I look around quickly and notice the absence of Kyron and his car.

"Skye, how far away do you live?" I ask.

"About a ten minute drive away, why?" She replies.

"Let's go!" I shout, "I think I know where to find him."

"I hope he hasn't!" She says as she starts her car, slams it into gear, and puts her foot down. "It will only make it worse for me."

"What do you mean?" I ask, as she swerves to avoid a parked car.

"I was moving the bedroom around one day and came across an old shoebox, which I knew wasn't mine. I didn't open it; I just rested in on the chest of drawers." She says, staring off into the distance. "He came home, saw the box, and just blew up. Pinned me against the wall by my throat, demanding to know why I had been snooping around." She finishes with tears in her eyes.

"Skye, has he ever hit you?" I ask cautiously. I don't want to sound judgemental.

"No, never," she says, confidently. "I remember after he pinned me up, I ran to my parents' house. Dad spotted the marks around my neck and he went crazy. He stormed round there demanding to know what had happened." She stopped; fresh tears were appearing in her eyes. Something tells me, what happened next isn't good.

Chapter 14

"Kyron! Long time, no see dude! How are you? Where's Skye? She said she was meeting you on the job." Elijah says, looking over Kyrons shoulder.

"She's probably on her way now," Kyron replies. "Can I come in?"

"Sure! My home is your home!" Elijah opens the door wider to allow Kyron to enter.

"Seems so long since I was here last, how long has it been? Three months? Six?" Kyron asks, looking around the living room. "I see you've had some new pictures taken."

"It's been a while, yeah." He responds.

Kyron thinks carefully about his next words before he speaks. Elijah doesn't seem too suspicious so there is no need to spook him just yet.

"No plans for kids yet Eli?" Kyron says, as if it's a normal icebreaker.

"Skye doesn't really want any," he responds. "After her parents passing, she says he doesn't want to put them through that if anything were to happen to either of us, especially with her job."

"Understandable I guess. She was close to her parents." Kyron says. "She was so upset when they died so suddenly."

"I remember it well, "Eli says. " Drink?"

"Water please, if you don't mind." Kyron replies.

We can see both men inside the house from our hiding place just outside Skye's' driveway.

"What do you think they are talking about?" She asks.

"Hopefully not the case. I don't want Kyron to frighten him away." I reply.

Between us, we decide that I will hide in the woods nearby, good job I know them well. Skye will go in and test the environment. If she senses something wrong then she will close the curtains and I will call for help. I climb from the car, wishing her luck. She looks so scared. I wonder if she always feels scared coming home, I make a mental note to ask her later. Skye creeps her car slowly up the driveway, then gets out, slamming the car door so violently the whole car shakes. She'd definitely make a great actress if all this police work falls through. All I can do know is wait and hope.

Opening the front door, Skye can hear chatter and laughter. Things seem calm, she thinks. Time for action.

"Eli?" She shouts. "Have you got company?"

"Hey Skye!" replies Kyron.

"Kyron! So, this is where you disappeared off to. I looked for you all over the scene! I know you said you would visit soon but I didn't think you meant so soon!" She says, sounding surprised. "I didn't see you car out front, did you walk here?"

"It wasn't far. I fancied a stroll. This new case is really hitting home," Kyron replied.

"It was a surprise to me too!" Eli exclaims. "Did you come back for something?"

"Yeah, I forgot to pick up the spare charger for my phone," she says as she goes up the stairs. "I've arranged for a take away to be delivered later if I'm not back in time to cook dinner, hope that's ok?"

"Sure, no problem babe!" Eli responds. "Take all the time you need. Seems like a big case." He laughs and looks over at Kyron. "She loves her job, doesn't she?"

"She's a brilliant detective, you should be proud!" he says.

"Indeed I am," Eli responds.

They hear her coming back down the stairs.

"I'm off now, I'll be back as soon as I can," she says, giving him a quick kiss on the cheek.

"I'll ride along with you Skye," Kyron says, quickly shaking Eli's hand. "We will meet up again soon." Kyron tells him.

"I look forward to it Kyron," he says. "We should all go out for dinner!"

I'd watched the exchange between them all and decided that everything seemed safe so I made a silent getaway. Having arrived at home, I could see that the forensics team were just clearing away; it was now a waiting game to see if anything else was found. I fill the kettle and pull a cup from the cupboard, drop a teabag in and wait. As soon as the kettle boils, there is a knock at the front door. I freeze. The knock comes again, slightly lighter this time. I turn from the sink and slowly walk to the door. I check the spy hole before opening it. There stands Kyron and Skye. I open the door swiftly.

"Kettle has just boiled, tea anyone?" I offer.

"That would be great," the both say in unison.

We sit at the table with our hands wrapped around our cups, trying to decide who will speak first. I am running things round my head; the timing of the letter is too much of a coincidence to when Kyron was here. Could he be part of it? Could they have passed each other in the street and not noticed? Surely, Kyron would notice him in the street. Maybe he was hiding in the bushes just off the porch way. That would be too close for comfort, especially since Mum is normally here alone.

"So how do we play along with this?" I ask.

"In all honesty Shea," Skye says, "I'm not entirely sure."

I take a deep breath and go back to thinking. We sit for a while longer and I tell them more about Jack, Jemma's folder, and the case that got us into this mess. After going over things at least three times it was getting way too late for anyone to fully understand the extent of everything. We decide to call it a night. I give Skye my mobile number and tell her to call if she needed to. I feel a pang of guilt watching her start her journey back to him. I tell Kyron to watch out for her, without disclosing anything that she told me earlier. That is her business to discuss when she is ready.

I receive a brief message from Skye later that night.

'All is well. Not to worry.'

At least I can rest a little easier now. I call Mum at Harriets, just a brief chat to let her know I'm safe. I can't tell her everything we've discovered tonight, at least not via phone,

I'll update her if needs be. Until then, its best she doesn't know. After reassuring her, for the fifth time, that everything was fine, I hang up and promise myself some well-needed rest. If that was ever going to be a thing again. I decide to take a soak in the bath, just to relax my body. Whilst I lay in the hot water, I go over everything in my head repeatedly. How didn't this police force recognise him? We had the whole country looking for him. We knew he had connections in Yorkshire and Manchester, but why didn't anyone notice him. Has he really changed that much?

'Stop dwelling on it now Shea' I scold myself.

At least I know where he was the whole time, but I wonder, is he still as dangerous as he was before? I needed to stop thinking for a while. I needed to recharge and make sure I was one-step ahead of him. I climb into bed and sleep claims me almost instantly.

Chapter 15

'Something seems familiar about my surroundings, like, I know exactly where I am. I don't normally recognise anything. Does this mean I'm starting to understand things more clearly?

"No, Shea, you have always been in the same place, you just see it for what it is now," Zephyr says.

"Why couldn't I see it before?" I demand.

"Shh!" Zephyr gestures. "He's still here, somewhere."

"Tell me! I don't understand," I ask.

"Look around," he says. "You never did that before, you just ran. You're not understanding things more clearly, just opening your eyes more, now GET DOWN!"

Just as he says that, Jack stomps past, eyes wide, searching all available hiding places. I swear he can hear me breathing; he stops and takes a deep breath.

"I can smell your fear Shea!" Jack booms, so close I can feel the floor rumble. "I know you're scared. She was too. Poor little Jemma, hahaha!"

I wish I could just grab him and shake the life out of him but I know I can't.

"Don't panic Shea," Zephyr says, sitting just next to me.

"I'm trying not to but he knows how to scare me, and I don't know how to not be scared," I say in a hushed tone.

He turns to his left. Something made a noise. I don't normally hear things in my dreams, just heavy breathing, and Jacks pounding voice. Could it be Zephyr causing a distraction so I can escape?

"That's not me," he says. "I can read your mind here."

Great!

"Run!" Zephyr says. "Run straight ahead, don't look back. Run towards the willow tree then take a sharp left straight to the oak tree."

I take off as fast as I can, reminding myself not to look back, left at the willow, straight to the oak, I chance a look back.

SKYE!'

I wake up in a sweat. How and why was Skye in my dream? I check my phone, it's 7:30am and there's a text from Kyron.

'Skye didn't show up for her shift. Sent patrol car past the house. All lights off. NO CARS IN DRIVEWAY. Currently worried.'

I quickly dial Kyron as I get dressed, it goes straight to voicemail. He must be driving; I'll try again in a few minutes. I hope nothing has happened. Just as I'm about to dial out again, Kyron calls, well saves me a job.

"Any news?" I ask, bypassing the morning pleasantries.

"Nothing yet. Did she contact you last night?" he asks.

"Only to tell me not to worry," I reply. "Why don't you come over and I'll show you. You probably know her text better than me."

"I'll be about 15 minutes. Just want to swing by Skye's; it looks less suspicious if I just drop in. I'll see you soon." He says and hangs up.

I go to the kitchen and put the kettle on. By the time he arrives the kettle should be done and tea brewing in the teapot. I glance at my phone just as it pings with an email. I use my laptop to access it and I'm shocked to see it's from Harriet. Why wouldn't she just call?

'Shea,

I'm emailing instead of calling, as I don't want to give this message over the phone. I feel I'm being watched, but I must tell you this. Your Mum wasn't in her bed this morning.

I didn't want to speak over the phone as Derek thinks she is still sleeping. Oh Shea, what do I do?

Sending love,

Harriet.'

How can she sit so calmly and write an email like that! She knows how vulnerable Mum is right now! I throw my shoes on and head to the door, all the while calling Kyron. He doesn't answer but I'm not surprised, I didn't expect him to. I leave him a brief message.

"Mum's missing too. Harriet emailed me! Call when you can." I say and hang up.

I open the door and almost sprinted to Harriet's door. I remembered she hid a spare key under the rock next to the strange looking gnome with the blue eyes. I swear that thing follows you wherever you walk. I unlock the door and almost run head on into Mum.

"Mum!" I scream. "Where's Harriet?"

"Right here dear, whatever is the matter?" Harriet says from the kitchen door.

"I got an email from you, you said Mum was missing!" I blurted out.

"I'm certain if something like that had happened, I wouldn't be emailing you dear. I'd be on your doorstep taking the door off its hinges!" she replies, still pouring the tea. "Come sit down darling, you look a fright!"

I allow myself to me guided, again, to the kitchen table. Harriet pours me some freshly squeezed orange juice. She says the acidity would kill off the shock. I hope she's right, I don't even think I can stand at the moment. Who would send an email like that? Then it hit me. Jack! He must have wanted me out of the house! He was watching my every move and that terrifies me.

I jump up way too fast for my brains liking. I sway slightly but regain my balance before hugging the floor. I rush out the door and collide with Kyron.

"Where's the fire?" he asks, looking confusingly at everyone including Mum.

"Jack! He's at the house!" I fling over my shoulder as I gain speed.

"Huh?" was the last thing I heard as I crashed through Mums front door and straight into something solid and sturdy. Then it went dark. Too dark. And quiet. Too quiet.

Chapter 16

"Where did she go?" Kyron shouts. "She was just here."

Lenora rushes into the house; stopping to take in the devastation that was her living room. She quickly took in the room, mentally noting if anything was missing. The TV was still there, so was the DVD player, even her Grandmothers wedding ring was still on the fireplace. Nothing seems to have been touched in here. She scans the kitchen and dining rooms, noting the drawers have been pulled out, and paperwork strewn all over the floor but still nothing expensive has been taken. She goes upstairs. As she walks up the stairs, she instantly knows where to look first. Sheas' bedroom. She takes a deep breath and opens the door, holding the handle tight to steady herself. Kyron rushes to her side and gasps at the sheer state of the room.

"Is it normally like this?" He asks.

"Absolutely not," Lenora snaps. "Shea is a very tidy person."

The once tidy, pristine room, with it neutral colours and blue splashed bed spread was now a picture of utter destruction. Sheas' clothes were thrown around the room, her suitcase upended on her bed. Lenora goes to the far side of the bed, knowing not to touch anything, she lifts the corner of the overhanging duvet with her foot, just enough to see Sheas' laptop bag and Jemmas folder still in their hiding spot. She knew what they were after, but they didn't have enough time to search properly before Shea sussed them out.

Kyron enters the room, he quickly looks around and calls forensics to come and do a once over,

"Anything obvious missing?" he asks quietly.

"No, they didn't have time to get what they came for," she responds, pointing at Shea's bag and the folder under the bed.

Kyron reaches down and picks them up.

"How much of this do you know about?" he asks Lenora.

"Enough to fill you in, but we will need Harriet too," she replies.

She calls Harriet to warn her that she and Kyron would be there soon to discuss Jemmas' folder and that if she still didn't want Derek to find out, she needed to give him something to occupy him for a while. Harriet is certain that it is time for him to know everything; she says she will set the table.

"Morning Princess!"

"What the?" I ask. Where am I?"

"Not sure yet," comes the reply again.

"Zephyr? Is that you?" I question again.

"10 points!" he replies. "Not so loud though, Sleeping Beauty over there keeps stirring and I don't know how to explain myself yet."

"Sleeping Beauty?" I ask, clearly aware that I'm blindfolded.

"Oh, sorry!" he says, removing the blindfold and shielding my eyes from the sudden influx of light. "Her." He says, pointing to the strange looking heap in the corner.

"Skye?" I ask, as quietly as I can but just loud enough for her to sit up a little. "Is that you?"

"Shea?" comes the reply. "I'm so sorry! I didn't mean for this to happen. He made me tell him everything. Well, as much as I knew."

"It's OK Skye, don't worry." I say back. "Kyron knows you're missing. I think he went to your house. Where are we and where is Eli?"

"For both questions, I don't know, but it smells like my basement, loads of old boxes and Dads old record collection. There's no electric down here so I couldn't say for sure," she says. "It's cold too."

"Zephyr," I whisper. "Can you do anything in regards to light?"

"I can try, but I'm still new to this magic stuff remember," he replies. "Hold on to your hair!"

POOF!

"Ah! Light!" He says proudly.

"Who..Who are you?" Skye exclaims, jumping back towards the wall.

"Oh, I'll let you deal with this one!" he says to me.

I let out an audible sigh. How to explain this one?

"OK, Skye, this is Zephyr," I begin. "Remember I told you about Jemma and how I was going to explain the folder to you and Kyron?"

"You were going to tell them?" Zephyr pipes up from the dark.

"Yes! I needed help!" I growl back.

"I remember vaguely," she replies, not taking her eyes off the shadows where Zephyr currently hides.

"Well Jemma used Moon Magic to summon Zephyr to my dreams as a way of protecting me. Only he can also sense my fear and appear in reality." I say.

At this point, Skye faints.

"Was that last part planned?" he asks me, looking down at Skye on the floor.

I just glare at him whilst trying to wake her up.

"I guess not." He says, answering his own question.

"Skye, come on, Wake up." I say gently, shaking her arm and resisting the urge to slap her awake. That wouldn't help anyone right now.

She slowly comes back to reality, and still looks visibly startled by this pale, red haired man beside me. She sits up straighter and adjusts her jumper. I can see a mark on her collarbone, it looks like a handprint or grab mark but I don't push her on it. I'll wait until she's ready to explain it, if she even knows it's there. I smile to her and carry on explaining about the magic, the folder anything else that ties in with all this. I just hope and pray that Jack didn't find the folder.

Chapter 17

Harriet sits everyone at the table, Kyron, Derek, Lenora, herself and Kyrons boss, Chief Inspector Troy Lysine. Lenora remembered him from Jermaine's time on the force. He was a lovely man. Harriet pours everyone tea, whilst Lenora quickly fills everyone in on what had happened up until now. Derek doesn't look too happy about being kept in the dark, but he understands why.

"Let me get this straight," Troy says, "Jemma and Shea were working the case of an abduction and assault when the defendant goes AWOL?"

"That's correct," Lenora replies. "No one could find him in the country so they assumed he had fled the country and changed his identity, which he had done but only fled up the country not out of it." She finishes.

"Jemma had issues from the day after the trial fell through, this was supposed to be the case to cement her career," Harriet says, looking sorrowfully at Derek.

"May I take a glance at her diary, actually, could I look at them both?" Troy asks.

Lenora passes him both diaries and he does a quick comparison. He comes to the same conclusion as everyone else. The same events on the same days. Could it be pure coincidence?

"How long did you say the girls had been friends?" He asks.

"Oh, wow, ever since they met at nursery, they were inseparable," Derek replies. "I remember that day like it was yesterday. Jemma was so happy to have found a friend on her own." He says, almost shedding a tear but holding it back at the last minute. Harriet, on the other hand, was dabbing her eyes with a crumpled up tissue the whole time.

"That's when we all became solid friends," Lenora says, gently rubbing Harriet arm. "Like one big family."

Harriet slides the sketch of Jack over to Troy.

"This is what Jemma drew. What she saw in her dream." She says, looking at Troy for some form of answer.

A moment of recognition flashed across his face. Harriet spotted it, as did Lenora.

"What is it Troy?" Lenora asks, clearly troubled by the look. "You recognise him, don't you?"

"I'm afraid so," he replies, not wanting to finish his sentence.

"It's Skye's husband, Elijah Coyle." Kyron finishes it for him.

Both Harriet and Lenora exchange glances. Derek looks blankly and both women.

"I'm sorry, but who is Skye?" he asks quizzically.

"She's my partner," Kyron responds. "She is currently missing."

"So is Shea, as of about an hour ago," Lenora adds.

"What? Well why are we just sitting around drinking blasted tea? She can't be that far away. We've already lost one girl to this lunatic, I'll be damned if he will take another form us!" Derek booms.

"Sadly, he already has." Kyron adds, explaining about Sierra.

"Oh that poor girls family!" He says, as he finally lets the tear fall that he'd held on to for so long. "Then we have to find him and the girls. He has to pay!"

Derek stood up, pulled his lumber jacket from the coat hook, laced up his black leather work boots, bid goodbye to everyone and off he went out the back door. He was determined to find them and bring them home.

Troy watched as Derek trudged off down the path on a mission to find them. He was impressed, but something bothered him.

"He won't know where to start?" he said, staring after him.

"Maybe not, but he knows this city better than anyone I know and he will explore and exhaust every known hiding place until he finds them," Harriet says, watching her husband with admiration.

I can hear footsteps above us, I gesture to Skye to keep quiet as I try to listen for voices.

"How could I not have found that stupid folder?" Eli says. I can't hear any replies so I guess he is by himself. "I bet she gave it back to that crazy old bat."

He must mean Harriet.

"Kyron will be looking for Skye everywhere. Good job I hid the cars! That nosey bloke was round here earlier asking all sorts of questions," he continues.

Who is he talking to? There is no reply to anything he's asking. This is so strange.

I crawl over to Skye and tell her what he is saying, trying to be as quiet as I can.

"Kyron came looking for you before he came to my house. I was going to show him the text that you sent me last night." I whisper.

"He has my phone," She whispers back. "He texted you last night, not me. I think he has an app installed on my phone somewhere that tells him where I am at all times and he can even listen in on everything within a certain distance. My phone is now a security risk."

"OK, we have to get a message to someone, somehow." I say, attempting to stay calm and think logically. What would Jemma do? Well, knowing Jemma she would just shout her life away in the hope someone hears her.

"We don't have any neighbours," she offers, without me needing to ask.

"I lost my phone earlier running from Harriets to my Mums' so there's no hope there." I add.

I let my mind wander for a while. Still listening to Eli pacing above. fourteen steps left, twelve steps right. I try to copy his exact pattern, memorising the different tones and echoes the flooring makes. After ten steps to the left, the floor sounds quieter. A rug maybe, I ask Skye.

"We have a shag pile rug near the coffee table. It's not huge bit it muffles sound," she replies.

When he walks back towards the right, I notice a different tone after eleven steps. Sounds like a trapdoor.

Chapter 18

"Oh Len, what are we going to do if we can't find them?" Harriet cried into her tissue.

Kyron and Derek had been gone hours without even a phone call or radio contact for update. Kyron had followed Derek within minutes. Troy had stayed behind to catch up on everything, have a good look through the folder, and make his own notes. With a seamlessly endless supply of tea, biscuits, and cake, he was satisfied he'd made the right decision.

"So," he says after what seems like an eternity but had really only been 3 hours. "This all started around 2 years ago when Jack abducted a young girl and then attacked her Mum. Do we know how the family are doing now?"

"Shea said she tried to stay in contact with them but when they stopped responding, she wasn't allowed to pursue it any further," Lenora replies.

"It does seem rather strange that they wouldn't be worried about the man who abducted their daughter still being on the run, I know if it was me, I'd want to be kept up to date," he says, in a matter of fact manner.

"We all would," Harriet says from the window, still standing by the phone waiting, almost pleading for it to ring. Then it did.

'RING'

"Hello? Derek is that you?" Harriet says into the receiver. "NO I DON'T WANT TO TALK ABOUT AN ACCIDENT IVE NEVER HAD!" and she slams the phone down, sobbing loudly.

"Mrs Summers?" Troy says, testing the atmosphere. "Why don't you and Mrs Hopewell take a stroll around the churchyard? I will stay here and wait for any news. I promise to come and fetch you both if there are any updates."

"That's sounds lovely Harriet, I'll fetch us both a cardigan." Lenora says excitedly, knowing exactly what Troy is up to, but nothing slips past Harriet that easily.

"We will go for half an hour, and then I will glue myself to that phone if I have to!" She replies sternly.

"Skye, you awake?" I whisper. "Skye?"

"Yeah, I'm awake, what's up?" She says back, sounding worried.

"He's gone out; at least I think he has. I heard him walking that way," I say, pointing to the left, "then I heard a door open and close but nothing after that."

"What did the door sound like? Did it creak?" She asks quickly.

"Just slightly, why?" I ask her, now beginning to get worried.

"He's gone to sleep in spare room downstairs. The front door doesn't make a noise and the back door is nailed shut," she says, so calmly.

Nailed shut? Who nails their back door shut?

"Hello Ladies!" Zephyr says and he just appears from nowhere.

"Can you try and warn me next time?!" I almost shout at him.

"Hey, listen, I only appear when you," he points at me, "get scared." He says.

"Right, dammit!" I reply.

"So, what got ya this time? Spiders?" he laughs.

"I'm not actually sure," I admit. "Skye just told me that the back door is nailed shut, why do you think it's like that?" I ask in a hushed tone.

"I think he's off his rocker," Zephyr says, like he is some sort of trained psychologist! "In fact, I'd bet money on it, but I don't have any to bet."

I have to admit, he does make me laugh with his little side digs, he reminded me of someone but I couldn't think who at this moment in time. I do wish he wouldn't just appear when I'm scared though, I could do with a friend to help me out of this situation. I don't even know how long we've been here. I'm cold, hungry, and tired; maybe I should follow Skye and get some rest. I'm sure Eli gave her something to make her tired all the time, but he didn't expect me to come back to the house so soon after the email so he didn't stock up for me. I can feel my eyes closing slowly. I curl up and sleep claims my thoughts. I can vaguely hear Zephyrs' voice.

"Goodnight Princess"

"I don't mean to sound impatient or anything Derek, but don't you think we should call home? Even if it is to say, there's no news? Kyron asks tentatively, he didn't want to anger Derek.

"Maybe after the next hill," Derek replies. "Harriet won't be happy with no news, but it's better than the alternative."

"I can't believe there's so much of this place I didn't know about," Kyron says, trying to make conversation. "Did you know I trained under Jermaine Hopewell?"

"That I did my boy," he replies. "He was my best friend, we spoke a lot about the recruits at the police academy, and he had high regards for you. Prove him right and find his baby girl."

Kyron knew he couldn't promise anything, but he could promise to do his best and try his hardest, even if it meant looking through the night. Natalie would understand. He quickly made a call to his wife, just to warn her that he will be either late or not home at all tonight. She understood, he knew she would, that's one of the reasons he married her, she was so understanding of his job.

At the next hill, Derek stopped to scan the area. It was getting late at gone 7pm. He decides to call home and update everyone. Kyron calls Troy to inform him that they will be searching through the night and asks him to just check on Natalie on his way home. Troy agrees reluctantly to them searching overnight, but promises to check on Kyron's wife.

"Harriet?" Derek says into the receiver. "I'm just calling to say we've had no luck. We will search overnight. Make sure you and Len rest.

Leave the worrying to us and lock the door when everyone leaves. I love you. Speak tomorrow."

"Ok darling. Be safe out there. Let me know where you end up and I'll bring you both breakfast." Harriet replies and hangs up. She knows Derek won't tell her where he is in the morning, but she likes to make the offer anyway. She takes the news to Lenora and makes another pot of tea.

They hadn't planned to stay out all night but they had to find them. No matter what the outcome was, Kyron owed it to Jermaine.

"So where next Derek? Surely it's going to be hard searching in the dark." Kyron says. "I've only got the torch on my phone and I don't think that will last very long at all."

"Don't worry boy," Derek replies, heading in the direction of what looks like a disused shed. "I know where to get supplies until morning."

He pulls out a small set of keys, finds the multicoloured key, and uses it on the door. It gently swings open to reveal a tavern of treasures to last them the night plus more.

"Here, take this." Derek says, passing Kyron a torch and several packs of batteries.

"Erm, I didn't come prepared to carry supplies," he gestures to his suit and no backpack.

"Good job we have provisions," Derek replies, handing him a red backpack. "Grab some of those chocolate biscuits and throw them in too."

Derek heads to the large white refrigerator at the back, pulls out 4 bottles of water, he puts 2 in his own back, and hands the other 2 to Kyron.

"Use it only when necessary, it needs to last all night. At least until 7am," he tells Kyron sternly. "It will be a long night if you don't."

"Why is all this here? Actually, more importantly, how LONG has it been here?" he asks worryingly.

"Jermaine and I built this when the girls were young. They liked to hide away from us and we were just preparing for the day they would get lost." Derek replies, letting his mind wander back to the good old days. "They never did mind you."

"You were both really close huh?" Kyron asks.

"That we were boy; that we were. I restock everything every 2 weeks. Just in case anything happens out here, bit like now." He replies looking at the picture of all 6 of them hanging on the wall. He salutes to his fallen friend and opens a map of the area on the small worktable. Kyron dips his head to the photo and turns to the map. Derek points out the church.

"We head there first. Afterwards we continue on to the woods here," he points out the wooded area just past the cemetery. "No scared of graves are you boy?" he asks.

"No sir!" Kyron replies, as if he is now back in training with Jermaine. "Under your order, I'm all good."

"Glad to hear it lad, let's head out." He says, handing him Jermaine's old coat.

Chapter 19

I wake up with a start and scan the surrounding room. Skye isn't here anymore. He must have moved her while I was asleep. How could I have slept through that? I always wake up to any noise. I'm a very light sleeper.

I look around and notice I'm not where I was before. Maybe it was me he moved and not Skye. I still don't understand how I didn't wake up. That's when I feel the pain in my neck. He injected me with some sort of sedative, of course, I'm not 100% sure, but what other explanation is there. I need to work out where I am, but it's so cold and dark here.

"Hello?" I shout. "Is anyone there?"

There's no response, I should have guessed there wouldn't be. It's so cold, I could just drift back off to sleep, but I fight against it. I know if I fall asleep with it being so cold, I may never wake up. I get up and walk blindly around, hands outstretched, I feel the coldness of brick. A chill runs through me. I can, now smell damp air. Almost like I'm near water or worse, underground.

"Zephyr!" I shout, hoping I'm scared enough for him to appear. Nothing happens.

I try to think back to the book on Moon Magic that Jemma left for me, but my mind goes completely blank.

Derek and Kyron search the churchyard and the woods but there is no sign of them anywhere. Derek was starting to get worried. He sat on the bench in the clearing of the woods and hung his head whilst thinking.

"Is there anywhere else they used to hang out?" Kyron asks, interrupting Dereks' thoughts.

"No," he replies sharply. "They were always in the same places, especially that tree." He says, pointing straight ahead.

Derek gets up to look closer at the tree. He shone his torch around the flooring of the tree. Kyron wasn't sure what he was looking for so he shone his torch too, it added extra light.

"Jemma used to leave little notes for Shea to find. I'm just checking to see if there is anything to help," Derek offers without question.

Kyron nods and continues to help with the search, which eventually ends with both men asleep at the base of the tree until 6:30am. Derek wakes first and checks his watch, he sighs heavily and makes his way to a clearer area to call

Harriet and update them, he doesn't even expect them to be awake yet so he prepares to speak to the answer phone, the one thing he despises, but a cheery voice answers.

"Hello, Summers' residence!" Lenora answers, brightly.

"Len?" Derek says. "Why so cheerful? Has there been news of Shea?"

"Derek! So lovely to hear from you. No, there's no news yet I'm afraid. I still have my...my fingers crossed," she stumbles with her reply.

This attracts Dereks' full attention.

"How's Harriet? He asks. "Still asleep?"

"Oh no, she's making us breakfast." She replies.

"Len, is someone else there other than you and Harriet? Someone who shouldn't be? Just say yes or no." He says, slightly sterner than before.

"Yes, bacon and eggs, definitely runny eggs, they are the best!" she replies. "I must go, I'm on tea duty"

"I'll be home soon Len, stay alert!" he says as he gangs up the phone.

"Someone is at the house," he tells Kyron. "I think it's him."

Kyron grabs his phone and calls Troy.
"Boss, someone is at the Summers' house." He tells him quickly.

"Derek says Mrs Hopewell confirmed it as well as stumbling over her words, this attracted his attention. I think he has gone back for the folder."

"OK, I'll send a unit over; I'll tell them to mention that there is still no news on Shea and that they were just checking the area for any suspicious activity, thank you Wetherby." Troy says as he ends the call.

"Troy will send a unit over; let's hope both ladies haven't been hurt. We have to get back to them." Kyron says, turning to face Derek.

"You head back. I'm going to keep looking. I owe Jermaine that much," Derek says.

"Stay in contact," Kyron replies as he passes the extra supplies back to him. "Report in every few hours. Please."

Derek nods in agreement. They part ways with a firm handshake.

Skye opens her eyes slowly. The light is blinding. She blinks a few times before realising she is in the backseat of Elis' car. She isn't tied up anymore, she can move freely. She sits up slowly and looks around; they are parked outside Mrs Summers house. She chances a glance in the front seat, in the hope that Eli may have left the keys behind. Bingo! Right there in the ignition! He either didn't plan to stay long, or didn't plan on her waking up so soon. She swiftly shifted her whole body into the drivers seat and without a moments hesitation and without chancing a look outside, she started the car and slammed her foot down on the accelerator. She had to get to the police station; she had to tell Kyron about Shea. She couldn't stop until she got there.

Chapter 20

Elijah spun around fast when he heard a car start. He convinced himself it was a neighbour but cautiously walked to the window to look. There he saw the back end of his car speeding away, weaving all over the road. From the left he saw the police car arriving. He starts to panic.

"Which one of you called them?" he demands.

"Neither of us, we haven't been out of your eyesight long enough, remember?" Harriet says, sarcastically.

"You!" he points at Lenora, "When they knock, you act normal, no heroics and no mention of me being here, understand? I'll be watching you!"

"Do I let them in?" She asks, nervously.

"Do what is natural for you, don't raise suspicion! It's not that hard to understand is it?" he says, bearing his teeth.

He runs up the stairs two at a time and places himself just out of sight, but in a position to see and hear everything.

'Knock Knock'

Lenora calms herself before answering, this is so much more difficult in reality than it looks in the movies, she thinks.

"PC Booth, WPC Ryles, how lovely to see you both. Won't you come in?" She greets them with a big smile.

"Thank you for the invitation Mrs Hopewell," PC Booth says with a broad smile, "but we just wanted to inform you that there is no news about your daughter to update you with at the moment, but we will be in the area for a while today, asking questions from neighbours, we will pop in a little bit later though." WPC Ryles continues.

"Ah," says Lenora, sounded defeated. "I do hope you find her soon, I am extremely worried for her. I'm not even able to sleep properly, I'm that scared."

"We understand Mrs Hopewell; we are doing all we can to find her." She replies with a gentle squeeze of Lenora's arm.

With that, Lenora closes the door and locks it again.

"You did well," Eli says from the top step. "Now where did you say that folder was? We don't want it getting into the wrong hands now, do we?"

"We didn't say where it was," Harriet says, dismissively. "You've been asking the same question for the past three hours and neither of us have told you. You don't scare me JACK!"

"DONT CALL ME THAT!" He shouts. "My name is Elijah Coyle."

"That might what you call yourself now lad," Harriet teases him, "but it isn't who you really are."

"Harriet, stop tormenting him," Lenora begs. "He still has Shea somewhere."

"I know that, Len, but the whole time he is here trying to scare us, the more time the police have to find her," Harriet whispers, watching Eli pace the landing, rubbing his hand over his hair.

Harriet was confident Derek would find her before the police did, but Eli didn't know Derek was looking for her.

Kyron finally made it back to town. He figured he would pull in at the station to see if there were any updates on them both. It was worrying him that no one had heard anything on Skye. He'd been trying to call Troy the whole way back but since their call in the morning, he had heard nothing. As he rounded the corner of the car park, he spotted Eli's car parked at a strange angle, as if it had been rushed. He parked up and ran inside.

"Any news on DI Coyle?" he almost shouts when he enters the building.

Everyone stops what they are doing and points slowly to Troy's office. Kyron makes his way, slowly, to the office. Preparing himself for the worst. He knocks gently and goes in when prompted. As he opens the door, a smile appears across his face. There, sitting opposite Troy, is Skye. As clear as a summers day, maybe looking a little worse for wear but she was alive, that's all that matters. Kyron bends down to give her a hug, she held on so tight, she was scared, he could feel her shaking, she tried to speak but Troy stops her.

"Not yet," he says. "Let the doctor take a look at you first."

She nods gently. The door knocks and the local doctor enters. Kyron and Troy step outside the office to give Skye some privacy.

"What the heck happened to her?" He demands. "You said you would call if you found her!"

"Well, we didn't exactly find her," Troy replies, trying to assert his authority over Kyron. "She crashed through the door just after I received a radio call from Booth and Ryles regarding Mrs Hopewell and Mrs Summers. They said Mrs Hopewell looked rattled but couldn't say anything about Eli. There was no sign of him or his car. That's when Skye burst in through the front doors, unexpectedly."

"In his car! It's parked outside!" Kyron raises his voice, causing other members of staff to look over at them. "That means he could still be there!"

Troy radios through to all available units.

'PROCEED WITH EXTREME CAUTION. GO DOOR TO DOOR TO MAKE IT LOOK LESS SUSPICIOUS. EXERCISE GENERAL SEARCH PROCEDURE ON ALL GROUND FLOOR ROOM AND EXTERNAL GARDENS. REMEMBER WE STILL HAVE ONE MISSING FEMALE.'

The doctor emerges from Troy's office and speaks to Troy.

"Just some mild concussion, nothing too much to be concerned with. She did mention that he had given her something to make her sleep but they could just be over the counter sleepers. If anything changes, call me." She says quietly.

"Thank you doctor," Kyron says.

She smiles as she leaves the two men to it.

Kyron is first through the door but can't think of what he should ask first, where Shea is, or what did he do to her? He just stands there like an awkward piece of furniture, out of place in a pristine room.

Troy passes by him and sits behind his desk. He calls his secretary and asks for a pot of tea and one of strong coffee, he feels they will need this to get through what Skye has to say.

As his secretary places the pots on the table along with 3 cups and some biscuits, she smiles at Skye.

"It's great to see you back," she says softly.

Skye smiles her thanks but doesn't trust her voice enough yet to speak. With that, she leaves.

"So Skye, where shall we start?" Troy asks in a calm and caring voice, much the same tone he had used with Harriet and Lenora yesterday.

"I...don't really know," Skye shakes, trying to take a sip of her tea. Kyron holds it to her mouth and she takes a slow sip and then smiles at him.

Chapter 21

"Dammit, she wasn't supposed to wake up yet! The box says 'lasts 6/8 hours'. It's only been 4!" Eli screamed.

"Who?" questions Harriet, trying to look out the window over his shoulder.

"Skye!" he throws back at her nastily. "You didn't really think I'd bring Shea back here did you?" he laughs, "You both really are crazy."

Lenora just broke down in tears; she was praying he hadn't hurt her when the door knocked again. Eli ran up the stairs, faster this time because Harriet threw the door wide open.

"Hello again officers, won't you come in this time, I've just made tea! Please don't let two old ladies drink alone." She insists.

The officers smile and accept the invite. They go into the kitchen and have a cup of tea, while drinking they take a slow wander around the ground floor of the house. Eli can see them from his hiding spot on the top landing. He prayed they would just leave. He needed to find Skye before she did anything stupid. The officers didn't find anything but Harriet is tempted to tell them to look upstairs. She stops herself, remembering that if he is arrested they may never find Shea and she is the closest thing to Jemma she has now.

The officers thank the ladies for the tea and their time but they warn them to be extra vigilant as they are a direct connection to this case and they could be targets too.

Once the officers close the door, Eli runs down the stairs out the back door, jumps the back fence, and is out of sight before they could both blink.

"That was strange," they say together.

I feel like I've been sat here for days, but I know it's only been a few hours, at least I think it has. I've been listening out for any noises. Rustling from animals, voices anything, but all I hear is silence. Deafening silence. I never thought I'd wish for him to come back, but right now, Id settle for any human company.

"Come on Shea, think!" I scold myself. "You're brighter than this!"

"That's not going to help you, you stupid girl!" The voice comes from behind me, but I can't see anyone there. I don't even recognise the voice.

"Who's there?" I ask, trying to sound braver than I actually feel.

I can't be that scared because Zephyr hasn't appeared yet, either that or I imagined him. I'm starting to question my own sanity now.

The voice lights a gas lantern and his face is illuminated. Jack!

"What do you want from me?" I ask, still no sign of Zephyr! Am I, really, not scared because I'm shaking like a tree in a typhoon here?

"Oh please! As if you don't know the answer to that already!" He says, close to laughter. "You girls messed up my life!

That money was meant to set Vanessa and me up for life. If Saskia hadn't involved the police and let them follow her, none of this would have happened. I wouldn't have had to kill four people!"

"Four people?" I ask, sounding confused. "I thought it was just Jemma and Sierra?"

"Sierra was supposed to be you!" he says angrily. "She wasn't supposed to die."

"Jemma was?" I ask. "Why?"

"Both of you were so keen to put me away." He shouts, ignoring my question. "I would have lost Vanessa for good."

"Wait, who is Vanessa?" I demand. Was she an old girlfriend? Someone who made him kidnap that little girl and demand money so they could live a good life.

"She is my daughter! The girl I ok was Vanessa," he looks directly at me, his eyes showing regret and remorse.

"That little girl was called Annalise, I remember from the court documents, Annalise Stark," I reply, but judging by the look in his eyes, I actually think he is telling the truth.

"Her mother lied, Annalise was Vanessa's twin, she died shortly after she was born," he says, sounding defeated as he sits on the floor with his back against the door. Definitely, no way to escape and I couldn't run even if I tried.

I sat down where I was and asked for the whole story; I was intrigued as to why the court documents were wrong and why they wouldn't have checked things out properly.

He looks at me and laughs.

"Oh, now you want to hear the whole story? You didn't care before!" he shouts.

I wonder where Zephyr is, surely, he can sense I'm scared now, I've no way of escaping, and I'm stuck in here with him.

Troy is still trying to coax out the whole story from Skye but she keeps zoning out, like she's still affected by the sleepers.

"Skye?" Kyron says. "What happened after I drove home behind you?"

She turned to him, eyes red from crying.

"He was waiting for me just inside the door, waiting for me to hang my coat up, for me to lock my weapon in the safe, for me to change clothes, and then he held me against the bedroom door by my neck, he screamed in my face and demanded to know everything about Shea," she said, in one breath.

"OK, that's great, now breathe," Troy says, with surprise. "That's a lot for one night."

"That wasn't all of it," she says quietly.

"What else happened?" Kyron says, getting angrier by the second.

"He told me he bugged my phone. Knew every case I was working on and overheard every conversation I had within a certain range." She stopped to take a breath.

"Slow down your breathing Skye," Kyron said, squeezing her hand gently. "We've got time."

"No we don't!" She shouted. "He's got Shea! He's taken her to my Dad's old deer hide in the woods. He's going to kill her, just like he did Jemma, Sierra and my parents!"

"What?" Troy and Kyron shout collectively.

Chapter 22

I waited for him to start talking. I'm not sure what name to use for him right now, Elijah or Jack. He must have changed it via Deed Poll to get a new driving license and everything. Why wouldn't he show up as wanted? Did he change it legally or just keep his head down? This is too much to comprehend right now.

"The girls Mum and I split up just after Annalise died," he says, so softly I had to strain to hear him properly. "She blamed me for her death even though the doctors proved she was too small to have survived."

"I'm sorry about Annalise, I had no idea. All the information named Vanessa as Annalise." I say, cautiously. "You didn't mention this to the police during your interview?"

"I tried," he says with a deep sign, so deep it could have come from the deepest vacuum of space! "Every time I corrected her name they gave me some snide remark about being mentally unstable. The psychiatric reports showed clear results. I'm as sane as a tree trunk."

I tried to remember the report, whatever he had drugged me with was slowly wearing off. I vaguely remember the police asking him about Annalise, and then I remembered! He was constantly saying 'Vanessa, her name is Vanessa'. The police report stated he was getting agitated easily. Now I know why!

"I'm sorry, I don't really know what name to use for you," I say bluntly. "When you said 4 people, I get Jemma and Sierra, but who are the other 2?"

"Skye's parents," he says, crying. "I didn't mean to, they found out who I really was. Her Dad came to me the day I hit her for moving my secret box. The one with all the pictures of Vanessa inside."

By this time he was sounding so remorseful, I had started to feel sorry for him, but then I remembered what my Dad had taught me. Don't let your emotions cloud your judgement.

"Why would you hit her for moving it?" I ask, trying to sound more professional.

"I thought she'd gone through it and found out who I really was," he says, tears streaming down his face. "She hadn't

but I flipped, I was scared. I had never loved someone as much as Skye, not after the girls Mum."

"How?" I ask, just one word. A simple word that almost, always, catches everyone off guard.

"Sorry?" he says.

There it is! This, by my judgement, and it's never let me down before, tells me it was an accident. I don't think he meant to kill Skye's parents, so I try again.

"How?" I ask again.

"About two weeks after we had the argument, I came over, knowing they were still asleep, I let myself in and turned on the gas cooker on," he recites, as if reading from a transcript. "Coroner reported Carbon Monoxide poisoning." He takes a deep breath. "Skye out it down to her Mum being forgetful, but I knew what it was. I knew it was me."

"Did you start the gas leak to kill them or just disorientate them enough, so that if they told the police, no one would believe them and blame the after effects of the gas?" I ask outright.

"They normally wake up around 8:30am. We were all supposed to be going on a picnic that day, so when Skye hadn't heard from them by 10am, she went over there. She could smell the gas but knew where to switch it off. That's when she found them, still in bed," he says, still with tears falling. "The post mortem showed sleeping tablets in their system, which was the reason they hadn't woken up."

This was starting to affect me more than anything. He knew their sleeping patterns, switched on the gas but only intended to mess with their recollection. To make them sound crazy so that no one believed them.

"OK, but can I explain something, just quickly," I say, in as calm a voice as I can muster now.

"Sure," he says, sounding exhausted.

"If you didn't run away on your trial date," I can see his muscles tensing but I continue anyway, "The court would have listened to your side about Vanessa, and no doubt, would have asked for proof of both girls births." I look him directly in the eyes. "At some point down the line, you could have been awarded joint custody of her."

No sound came from him, just the sight of his shoulders rising and falling from the sobs.

Troy, Kyron, and Skye all bundle into Kyron's car. From the passenger seat, Troy dials Dereks' mobile number form Kyron's phone. It just rang and rang.

"Keep trying." Kyron demands.

"I am," Troy says, trying to make his voice carry more authority.

"Will you both please stop trying to better each other? We are all equal at this point in time!" Skye says from the back seat. "It's becoming childish."

Kyron and Troy both look at each other and shrug. The phone rings twice, three times, four times.

"Kyron? What's up?" Derek finally answers.

"Mr Summers this is Troy Lysine. We have a location for Miss Hopewell." He states.

"Well don't keep me in suspense lad!" Derek says. "Where?"

"I'm not sure on exact coordinates, but DI Coyle says he Dad had a deer hide out in the woods, she says he has taken Miss Hopewell there. Have you seen anything similar on your travels?" he asks, sounding hopeful.

"I've not passed one yet, but it looks like I could be coming up on something. A surrounding description could help." Derek says sarcastically.

Troy passes the phone over to Skye.

"He's asking for a description of the surrounding area," he says when she gives him a questioning look.

"Hello Mr Summers" she says softly.

"Ah, DI Coyle, lovely to hear your voice my dear, now, what's in the area surrounding your Dad's deer hide?" he asks with empathy. "Don't rush yourself."

"Its covered with a brown camouflage tarpaulin, the last time I was there, to the left of it, was a huge tree stump," she says, trying to remember every detail. "The door! It's red! Like fire!"

"I've found it!" Derek says. "There's voices coming from inside. I can make out Shea, she's alive!" he tries to sound excited without giving himself away.

"Fantastic! Send the co-ordinates to Kyrons phone and we will meet you there!" Skye says before ending the call.

"I take it, he found it?" Kyron says, looking at her through the rear view mirror.

"Yeah, he's sending the co-ordinates to your phone. But we have to get their quietly." She says with a small smile.

Chapter 23

"Could I still do it?" he asks, quietly.

"Do what Jack?" I ask, using his original name for the first time.

"Go to court for everything and still be able to see her?" He says, not mentioning her name. "I don't care how long it takes; even a letter from here would be enough, a constant contact."

"I couldn't say for sure, you've essentially killed 4 people, accidentally or not, could you handle the sentence that could possibly be handed down to you?" I answer, as honestly, as I can, trying to keep a clear head, just in case this is some form of trap.

"I would do anything to hear from Vanessa again," he says, more tears collecting in his eyes. Will you help me?" Well! I was not expecting that bit! Where did that come from? "Please help me; you're the only one who can."

Troy punched the numbers on to Kyron's sat nav and they all made their way slowly and quietly towards the hide. It was a fair distance into the woods from where they had parked and Kyron wondered if they would find it before nightfall, but just as they rounded a large oak tree, they could just make out Derek in the distance. He raised his arm to show his exact location.

They reached him in no time. It was so quiet considering the main road ran right behind them.

"Any movements?" Troy asks, in a hushed voice.

"None as yet, I've heard parts of the conversation but nothing that makes any sense to me," Derek replies.

"I'm going around the other side. Skye, stick by Dereks side," Kyron announces. "I mean it!"

"Yes sir!" She salutes.

Kyron make his way around to the far side. The hide didn't look like it had any windows from where they were before, but he could just make out a mudded window. There was enough light from the inside to produce a big built shadow, standing just taller than the second shadow which had just come into view. He contemplated barging through the door, but then quickly extinguished the thought; anything could happen to either of them inside if he did that. He was about to shout orders to the come out with their hands up but troy got to him just in time.

"Derek has a plan," he says. "He has a listening device that he is going to try and place close to the door. We need to know who is in there before we act."

"Good idea, remind me to ask him where he got it from," Kyron responds. "Who is going to put the device in place?" He asks, afraid of the answer.

"Skye, and before you throw all your toys out of your pram, it's because she is smaller and lighter than any of us!" Troy says quickly.

"OK but we cover her. I'm not losing her!" he responds.

They both make their way back to Derek and Skye. Derek looked up and nodded that he understood there would be questions later regarding the device. He wouldn't lie to them, he would tell them he brought it on the dark web but that would be it. While Derek explained to Skye how to get the device activated, Kyron searched the area for traps or any signs of backup. He found nothing.

"You ready young lady?" Derek asks Skye.

"As I'll ever be Sir," she replies, swallowing hard.

"Remember, it's only dangerous if you get caught, but we are all here, we won't let that happen." He says, kissing her forehead as he would if this was Jemma.

She smiled shyly, took a deep breath, and stepped slowly towards the door. She looked back once towards the three men protecting her and suddenly felt more confident than ever. She straightened her back and focused on the task trusted to her. Taking the last few steps, she flipped the switch on the device, placed it carefully by the door but not in the path of anyone entering or exiting, and slowly made her way back to the three men smiling.

"Let's see if we can pick up anything on this monstrosity," Derek says jokingly.

He tuned into the device and there was a slight noise, he tuned it some more, turning dials left and right, until it suddenly sprang to life. That's when they heard the voices.

"Shea, please. You are the only person left that can help me," Jack pleads with me. "I don't even care how long I spend in prison. I didn't mean for any of this. I didn't plan to kill anyone really."

I could see some form of remorse in his eyes, but could I really believe him. After everything that has happened.

"Firstly, tell me what happened with Jemma? Why was there blood everywhere?" I ask, not because I want to know but because I need to watch his reaction before I make my decision.

He sat down again. He took a deep breath and looked deep into my soul. I suddenly wished I hadn't asked and now I felt completely open to his story.

"The night it happened, I was in the back garden of her parents' house, I didn't have a plan as such," he begins, still looking directly at me. "I used the trellis to climb into her bedroom. I could hear her shouting, I couldn't work out what was being said, I got in through the window," he stops, but doesn't look away.

"What did you see?" I nearly didn't ask.

"She was sleeping, but now I could hear her shouting 'run Shea, he's coming'," he was still staring at me. He hadn't looked away once. Sure, he'd blinked a few times but his eyes were darting around looking for the next part of the story. "She never said who was coming, I tried to wake her up, to try and snap her out of it, she sat straight up, eyes wide and holding a hunting knife," his eyes remained on me the whole time. "I tried to take it from her but she recognised me just as the light from outside hit my face. She tried to scream but I held my hand over her mouth. She stopped for a second so I moved my hand. She didn't scream, she didn't blink, and she just fell back onto her pillow. That's when I saw what had happened. Somehow the knife had turned and sliced her throat." He stops, tears running like a tap down his face. "I honestly didn't mean to."

I, for once, was speechless. How do I even respond to this! If I were in court I would be inclined to believe what he was saying but Jemma was my best friend, my sister, my twin, well sort of, but you get it right? This man killed her, but could it have been accidental? Why was Jemma sleeping with a hunting knife? I had hoped this would give me answers, not more questions.

"Jack?" I say, quietly so I don't startle him too much. It had been so quiet since he stopped talking, I didn't know whether to speak or just stay silent. "Hey, if I help you, and that's a very big and important IF, you have to do everything the judge tells you to. I can represent you, but only if you agree." I say, using the most dominant voice I can.

Jack seems to take a few minutes to decide what he will do. I let him have a think over things, I can't go far, but I can't invade his space either.

Chapter 24

Kyron turns to look at Derek, his head in his hands silently sobbing. Kyron looks between his boss and his partner and suddenly it hits him. They all have tears in their eyes, including him. Skye puts her arm around Derek, who promptly sobs even more only now it is into Skye neck.

"It's Ok Mr Summers, we all heard it and we are all so deeply sorry you had to hear it too, especially like this." She whispers gently. "We will arrange someone to contact you when all this is over, they can help."

He nods and slowly lifts his head.

"Thank you," was all he could manage.

Troy cleared his throat, he looked between his colleagues, and he would arrange help for them too.

"So boss; what's our next move?" Skye asks boldly.

Troy just stares at her. Unaware of what to do in this situation. Judging by the atmosphere inside the hide, Shea was not in any immediate danger. She seemed to be in control.

"We wait," he replies. "Shea seems to have the upper hand. We can continue to listen in, if you all think you can handle it. I will understand if you can't."

"I'm sure the worst is over now," Derek says, wiping the remainder of his tears away. "Let's continue to listen, there may be extra information."

They stand; shoulder to shoulder to listen for more.

"I swear on Vanessa's life, I will serve my sentence, undertake and programmes given to me, anything for a part in my daughter's life, please," he says in a defenceless voice.

I considered him for a second or two. In fact, it was probably a whole minute. I still had no idea how I was going to do it.

This man had killed 4 people and threatened to kill me. The only thing I could think of was Jemma. What would she say? She would probably say I was completely insane to even be considering it, but I was. I think I have definitely lost my marbles! I take a deep breath in, trying to calm my nerves. This guy scares me to my core. Why isn't Zephyr here? I need to think but it's too cramped in here. Speaking of here.

"Where are we Jack?" I ask, testing the water, so to speak.

"Skye's Dad built this about 6 months before he died," he replies. "I couldn't leave you in the basement any longer, it wasn't fair."

He's talking about fair! Wow!

"Fair!" Kyron nearly screams luckily they all clamp their hands over his mouth just in time.

"We get that you're angry lad, but button it!" Derek hisses. "We all want her out alive, we get it!"

"Sorry," he says, half muffled by Derek's hand.

They carried on listening for a few minutes more. Derek's mobile vibrated in his pocket, he took it out and checked the caller ID, it was Harriet.

"Any news darling?" She asks, hopefully.

"We found her, she's alive." He whispers.

"Why are you whispering?" She demands.

"We are outside Skye's Dad's old deer hide in the woods; I'm using that listening device. We can hear everything they are saying," he says quickly. "I'll call you back soon, I love you." He hangs up quickly before she could say anything else.

"Trouble in paradise?" Troy asks, half giggling.

"If she starts, she won't stop until she's found us and brought her rolling pin." Derek replies.

"Dangerous!" Troy smiles, his own wife much the same.

"Of course! It's stainless steel!" Derek says with a chuckle.

"Have you both finished?" Kyron says impatiently. "Some of us are worried about Shea!" As soon as he had said it, he instantly regret it.

Derek grabbed him by the front of his shirt and lifted him off the ground. His face red from anger, he pulls Kyrons face close so they are eye to eye.

"Shea is the closest thing to a daughter I have now. Do you think this is easy for me to endure DCI Wetherby?" he says clearly.

"No, no sir!" Kyron responds, his voice clearly shaken. "I meant no offence sir."

Derek places him back on the floor, Kyrons legs nearly buckling underneath him.

"I'm sorry lad!" Derek says, trying to hide his face away.

"No, I'm sorry. I didn't engage my brain before I spoke," Kyron replies.

"That's enough testosterone!" Skye says, "You're missing it all."

"So what happens now?"

"Zephyr!" I cry, "You do pick your time!"

"Sorry!" he smiles. That smile. It's a shame he isn't real.

"Nope!" he says. I instantly blush. I forgot he could read my mind!

"What in the name of all that is holy is that?" Jack says, hyperventilating.

"Don't panic Jack," I say in a gentle voice. "He won't hurt either of us."

"So! You're the one! I thought I recognised you!" Jack says, calming down a little.

"Sorry, how?" Zephyr replies, cockily. He knew, perfectly well, how!

"You...It can't be." Jack was murmuring something about the woods.

"I changed the layout, yes. You got lost. One point for you," Zephyr says, playing around with him. Not good at this point in time.

"Zephyr, please. That's enough." I say, sternly. "Jack has agreed to pass his time in prison for everything he has done."

"Oh good for him!" He replies sarcastically, clapping his hands silently.

"Please," Jack says. "I just want contact with my daughter."

Zephyr grabs my arm and pulls me as far from Jack as he can, which isn't far considering how small this place is. In any other circumstances, I would have loved to be away from this creep but not now, I needed to keep a close eye on him.

"Are you really going to let him go? After everything?" He asks quietly.

"I genuinely believe him," I reply. "I believe he just wanted to be with his daughter. You should have been here when he was telling me about Jemma. His eyes never left mine."

I know. I was watching through your eyes." He admits. "I've been here the whole time, but I just needed to see the brave Shea."

That's so strange to hear. My Dad used to call me that. Guess it's as common as he said it was!

"What do I do now?" I ask. "I can't believe you let me think I was alone!"

"You're never alone Shea, but this is your party. What do you want to do? I'm behind you every step of the way," he says with a glint in his eye.

I knew what to do.

Chapter 25

"Who is Zephyr? I didn't see anyone go past me!" Troy says, nearly exploding on the spot. "Kyron, you said only 2 shadows showed up in the blacked out window!"

Kyron looked around worryingly. Did he really miss another shadow? Did someone slip past him without him seeing? Surely not.

"No one passed anyone boss, I can promise you that," Kyron says.

"Ha ha, of course no one did," Skye says, giggling to herself. "Shea hasn't had a chance to introduce us all yet, but it's not my party trick to share lads, sorry." She shrugs, turns away, and smiles to herself. She can't wait to see their faces.

"The name does seem awfully familiar," Derek says, deep in thought. "I'm sure I heard Jemma say it once or twice, I could have been dreaming mind you."

This sparked another giggle from Skye.

"She knows something!" Kyron says angrily. "Is she in trouble?"

"Oh Lord no!" Skye says. "Just wait for her to share."

"Listen" Troy whispers.

"Jack? You still with me?" I ask gently. I have concluded that the gentle approach is best for him. There's too much shouting and screaming going on, or is that in my head?

"Hmm? Oh yes sorry," he replies. "What's our action plan?" He asks, looking between Zephyr and me.

"Do you know how to get back to town from here?" I ask, slowly.

"As long as he doesn't change anything then yes." He says, pointing at Zephyr. "Are we going straight to the police station?" he asks, in rapid questions.

Zephyr won't change anything," I promise him. "We have to go though; this has to happen now, before you change your mind again."

He nods his understanding and starts to rise from the floor. He looks at me with sad eyes. Its hit him that this could be his last day of freedom for at least 20 years, so I don't rush him. Zephyr looks on between us both with a smile; he understands why I'm doing this and it isn't to forget about Jemma, or Sierra or Skye's parents. It's to allow the passage of grief to free their souls, to allow them to pass on peacefully.

"Take your time Jack. I'm worried about you." I say.

"Why?" he says, a little caught off guard.

"You ran last time. How do I know you won't run again?" I ask.

He looks at me head on and says, "I was scared."

A genuine answer from a man who actually looks terrified.

"When I was young, I was bullied for being a slow learner, so when I met Saskia, I was in shock. When she had the girls, I was so happy, but when we lost Annalise, she turned nasty," he says with tears in his eyes. "She would laugh at me and call me names, hurtful names. She would say she was with me out of pity."

I could see it more now with every word he spoke about his childhood and into adulthood. He was scared of people calling him names. He wanted to prove he wasn't those names.

"Jack, have you ever had any tests about your learning?" I ask, choosing my words carefully so as not to scare him.

"What do you mean? Mum said it's because I'm think, that some people are born thick." He replies a little shaken by the question, but shrugs when he mentions what his Mum said.

"It's nothing to worry about," I say as I held his arm, "but we can check some things out at the police station."

I guide him to towards the door.

"Skye, is anything wrong with Elijah mentally?" Kyron asks.

"Not that I'm aware of," she replies with a worried look on her face. "He isn't always the brightest bulb in the chandelier but I never thought it was anything to worry about."

This wasn't what they needed to hear right now. If he really was mentally ill, they could all be in danger.

"The door." Derek points ahead. "Get down!"

They all sank to the ground, the long grass just tall enough to hide them from view.

"Who came out?" whispers Kyron.

"No one yet." Troy replies.

They all stare at the door as it slowly opens wider. They all catch a glimpse of the flame red hair; they pale skin and the darkest eyes they've ever seen.

"Zephyr," whispers Skye, in awe of his appearance in daylight.

"That's Zephyr?" Kyron asks, still confused over who this guy is.

Oh yes!" Skye replies, unable to take her eyes off him.

"He's almost unreal." He says, avoiding her eyes.

Skye didn't let on but she just imagined if he were real, he definitely wouldn't be without a lady on his arm, that's for sure. He really was something to look at. Even Troy was speechless, that never happens!

The three men just watch as Zephyr almost glides away from the door. He looks around, checking out the area. He heads in their direction but there is nowhere left for them to hide. As Zephyr spots them, he dips his head in silent confirmation that their secret is safe. He then moves silently back towards the door.

"All clear on the western front Captain!" he says, giving me a long salute. He's absolutely crazy, but he's great at it too!

"Fantastic, thank you." I reply. "All ready Jack?"

"Me? Yes, I think so, yes I'm ready, yes definitely ready." He says nervously.

I hope this works, I'm terrified of it all going wrong. I will look so stupid but I have to give him a chance, he clearly needs help. I take his arm and we slowly make our way to the doorway. He stops just before the door. 'Oh please don't back out now' I think to myself.

"Before we go, I just want to say something," he says, turning to look at me. "I want to say thank you."

"Why are you thanking me? I should be thanking you for letting me help you," I say, getting a little teary eyed.

"No, your offer of help is what I've probably been doing all this for. I just wanted someone to listen." He says.

He starts to walk again, this time more confidently. He knows he needs help, which is good. Although too late for Jemma, Sierra and Skye's parents, hopefully it's not too late for him, Skye and, fingers crossed, Vanessa.

Chapter 26

From their hiding place. Kyron and Troy try to work out the best way to take Elijah down, without causing harm to him or Shea.

"I could try to get behind him and take him down that way?" Kyron whispers.

"Won't work," Derek interrupts them, "He's looking around, and none of your plans will work."

"Which way did he come in? I didn't see any other cars when we parked up," Troy says, realising they hadn't seen another single person since they arrived.

"There's another entrance on the far side. Closer to his house, he must have come that way," Derek says, he knew these woods well.

Skye's gaze never left her husband and Shea. She watched his every move, she hoped she knew him well enough to know if he was about to turn. She couldn't figure out how she didn't notice how slow he was learning things. Sure, he struggled to read, she knew that, but she had never seen he husband this helpless before. He was always showing strength and confidence. Why wouldn't he ask her for help? She decided that she wanted to help him too. She had her own idea on how to bring him in, without the men interfering. She slowly slid as far from sight as she could before standing up behind a large, broad trunked tree, she was far enough from them and close enough to the entrance to run if she needed to without giving away their location. She took a deep breath and shouted.

"Elijah! Elijah where are you?"

"What? What is she doing?" Kyron shouts, almost giving them away again. "How did she get there without us knowing?"

"Taught by her Daddy I expect," Derek says sounding proud of her initiative to handle it her way. Elijah was her husband after all.

"Wow!" was all Troy could say.

They watched how Elijah reacted to her voice. He seemed to calm down a little.

"I'm here Skye!" he shouts back. "I'm near your Dads deer hide. I have Shea with me."

"I'm coming. Is everything alright?" She replies, picking her way carefully towards them.

When she reaches them both, she smiles at them, gives Shea a quick hug, and then pulls her husband in for a longer hug. She holds on tight.

"What's wrong?" he asks her, he looks worried.

"Nothing. I was just so worried about you," she replies, rubbing his arm.

"You drove off!" he says, starting to raise his voice.

"I was scared baby," she says quietly. "You were scaring me, you put me in the basement, and then you kidnapped Shea. I was terrified. I'm sorry."

He pulled her close again.

"No, I'm sorry," he cries in to her shoulder.

Skye looks at me over his shoulder.

"You OK?" she mouths.

I nod. Feeling better in knowing she's alright too.

"Shall we get going Jack?" I prompt.

"Jack?" Skye questions.

"Don't play dumb babe, I know you know who I am really," he says. "I understand if you want to leave me, I'm a complete mess and I need fixing."

"I'm not going anywhere," she replies. "Where are we off to?" She knew where, but she couldn't let on.

"I'm going to hand myself in to the police. I have to serve my time for what I have done," he says, starting to explain everything.

"Jack, there will be plenty of time for you to explain later; I will make sure you both have some privacy." I say, urging him to carry on walking.

"Shea is going to help me; so I can see Vanessa again," he says proudly.

"Who is Vanessa?" she asks, again, knowing the answer but playing dumb.

Later Skye," I say, giving her a look that tells her to stop asking questions.

"Oh yeah, sorry. I have a lot of catching up to do," she says, taking hold of his other arm.

We walked just a few more meters until we were practically in Skye's back garden. It must be amazing to have all this on your back step. Jack was quiet the whole walk back, except for the odd squeal of excitement from seeing a squirrel. It really surprised me at how excited he got.

"Haven't you seen one before?" I ask, as we get to the edge of the garden fence.

"I don't venture out much," he admits. "I find it hard. I can open the door, but then I freeze, unless I'm with Skye, then I can make it out and about." He says, looking at Skye with admiration. I can clearly feel the lump in my throat.

"Skye, do you have any nuts in the house?" I ask.

"I'm pretty sure we have some somewhere. Ill grab some," she replies, clicking on to my thinking.

"Come and sit here Jack," I gesture to the garden bench; I guide him to sit down.

Skye comes back about two minutes later with a bag full of nuts. She nods at me and I know that she has called the others to make them aware that we are alright. I place some nuts in the palm of Jacks hand and make a tutting noise with my tongue.

"What are you doing?" he asks, nervously.

"Just wait quietly and see." I reply.

As I say those words, two squirrels appear.

"Shh," I gesture, lowering his hands to ground level. They spring forward carefully. Stopping just short of his hands to have a sniff around. I can see him trying to control his excitement. One of them jumps forward and takes some nuts from his outstretched hands. The smaller of the two is a little more hesitant but eventually does the same; only he lingers a little longer, having a bite of one whilst sitting in Jacks hand. Jack looks down and smiles, a gentle smiles, his eyes filling with tears. Eventually, Jacks hands are empty and he is left with a smile so wide it almost doesn't fit his face anymore.

"That might be the only time I will ever be able to do that," he says softly.

"Don't think that way, remember, positive thinking." I say to him. "That's the only way."

Chapter 27

Make sure we have a therapist ready, and stock up on tea, coffee, and snacks, it could be a long night," Kyron says to Troy's' receptionist. He then ends the call.

"Time to head back," Troy says. "Can we drop you home Derek?"

Derek looks around the woods a little longer and then nods. "That would be great, thank you."

They make their way back to Kyron's car. Along the way, Derek remembers times that he and Jermaine would trek through here and take different paths around, how they would bring the girls and watch them climb trees. Jemma wasn't so good, she was a little girly girl, but Shea would scamper up the tree like a cat being chased by a dog. She tried to help Jemma but it just wasn't to be. He chuckles to himself; the other two don't seem to notice. A story to share with Harriet and Lenora when he gets home. He then realises he hasn't called Harriet back, he pulls out his phone but then decides to let it be a surprise.

"I wonder where they are!" Harriet says, impatiently pacing back and forth in front of the big bay window in the living room.

Shea had called from the police station to say she was safe but that she had something to do before she came back.

"You will wear that patch of carpet out if you keep pacing like that! Derek will be back before you know it," Lenora says, sitting on the sofa trying to finish a crossword she started two hours ago. She was adamant they were getting harder, either that or she was losing her touch.

"What could be taking so long?" Harriet demands. "Derek should be home by now!"

"Probably lost track of time in the woods," Lenora replies.

A car rolls up outside the house. Harriet almost rips the door off its hinges to get to Derek, who she spots climbing from the rear door.

"Where have you been? I've been so worried," she says, running into his outstretched arms.

"There was no need to worry love. I was perfectly safe," he says, holding her a little closer than normal.

"Did you see Shea?" Lenora asks. Even though Shea had called but 2 and a half hours ago, she needed to be sure someone had seen her safe and well.

"She's fine Len. You would have been so proud of her out there," he replies with a tear in his eye. "I was!"

Lenora looks up to the sky and says, "We did good Jermaine, we did good with our baby girl."

"Will you ladies excuse me; I'm going for a shower and change of clothes. Thanks for the lift home gents!" Derek says and he heads in the front door and up the stairs. He feels a pang of guilt that his best friend didn't have a chance to see how brilliant his daughter was in the situation. He let the tears silently fall as he showers.

"Will he be alright?" Kyron asks from behind them, nodding in the direction Derek had left.

"Only time will tell," Lenora replies. "Jermaine and Derek were so close. Derek feels he has a duty to keep us both safe, for Jermaine's sake."

"Well, you both have our numbers if you need us at any time," he says as he turns to leave.

"Thank you for everything," both women say together with a smile.

Once he composed himself, Derek makes his way to the kitchen where Harriet and Lenora are still trying to finish the crossword.

He peeks over his wife's shoulder, reads the clue, and says "PERFECT!"

"I beg your very pardon?" Lenora asks.

"Something without flaws," he replies.

"I swear that says something which flows," she replies, squinting at the page.

Derek chuckles to himself. He wouldn't have Len any other way.

"Would you both mind if I quickly went out again. I won't be long," he asks.

"You never need permission, you know that," Harriet replies with a squeeze of his hand.

Lenora feels a stab of jealousy in her heart. She missed Jermaine more than anything now, but she silently promised him to get treatment and survive, if only for the sake of Shea.

Derek reaches the graveside, lays his flowers, and places himself on the damp patch of grass beside Jermaine's headstone.

"You would have been so proud of her Jay," he says, trying not to cry. "She did so well in there with him. I know you would have burst in there to save her, I should have too, but hearing how she handled herself, really reminded me of you. It brought a lump to my throat."

Derek closes his eyes for a brief minute to compose himself, but when he opens them, stood in front of him is this pale-faced, red haired man.

"I know how you feel Derek, she did well. I was there the whole time," the figure says.

"Who, or what, are you?" Derek stutters.

"You may have heard Shea call me Zephyr," he replies.

"Ah, yes I did, but what are you exactly?" Derek asks.

"You know WHO I am really. There is so much to explain but not until Shea has finished what she has to do. Even then, she can't know who I am," he says with a tap of his nose.

"Jay?" Derek asks surprisingly.

"Shh! Just promise me you will look after Len and Shea for me. I will appear to her now and then, but I want you to look out for them, as I am with Jemma on this side. It will be hard to understand D, but I can only do this with Jemma's help." He explains as much as he can.

"I promise," is all Derek can muster. At least he knew Jemma and believed Jemma was safe and not alone.

Nothing really spooked Derek; he had an open mind and believed anything was possible. He looked up again and Zephyr was gone. Derek stands up, taps the headstone, and makes his way home.

Chapter 28

When they arrive at the station, Shea, Jack, and Skye are all taken in to a side room. Not quite as small as an interview room, but about the size of a small conference room.

"How long do we have this room for?" I ask Skye.

"As long as we need it for," she replies holding Jack's hand tight.

He looks like a child about to be taken to the dentist for the first time; he looks at the table, between each chair and then walks to the chair furthest from the window. He sits down, Skye sits next to him on the left, and she watches him and shows so much love towards him, it reminds me of how

Mum used to watch Dad when he didn't know, she would watch how he reacted to the TV, this was exactly how Skye was watching Jack.

"Would either of you like a drink?" I ask.

"Tea, please, if you don't mind, milky, one sugar," Jack replies.

"Skye?" I prompt.

"Same please," she says, not taking her eyes off him.

"Sure, I won't be long," I say as I leave to get the drinks.

"How are you feeling?" Skye asks him. "I don't even know what name to use for you at the moment."

"I'm not sure how to answer that at the moment Skye," he replies. "I'm hardly sure I know who I really am."

"I won't push you. I'm here for you no matter how long it all takes," Skye tells him.

He allows himself to accept her arms, but is careful enough not to let it distract him from what he needs to do.

"Boo!"

"Argh!" I screech. "Zephyr!"

"Surprise!" he says with a smile.

"Not to be rude or anything but, why are you here?" I ask, trying got keep my voice low. "I'm not scared."

"I know you don't think you are, but why else would I be here? He replies with a wink of his eye. He reminded me of someone when he did that. Strange though, because I can't think who.

"Ok, maybe I am a little apprehensive about how this is all going to play out. I don't want Jack to back away from this. He needs this. So do Derek and Harriet. So do I!" I reply.

"It will all be fine Shea, stop getting all negative on me," he says, still smiling.

I grab the tray of drinks and make my way back to Skye and Jack. As I round the corner, I hear Troy and Kyron talking in hushed voices.

"Do you think Shea should really hear all this? Kyron says.

"Jemma was her best friend Ky, she needs this as much as anyone else," Troy replies.

"I get that, I really do, I just think she may have gotten herself too deeply involved in it all," Kyron says back.

He really doesn't understand at all does he? It's not just about Jemma. It's about Sierra too; her family deserve to know why she died. It's only fair.

"Stupid tray!" I say, loudly enough that Troy rushes to help me.

"Let me take that for you," he offers, plucking the tray from my hands.

"Thanks" I smile. "I didn't know you had both arrived otherwise I would have got you both a drink too."

"I thought my receptionist was sorting all that," he says, giving Kyron a sideways glance. "Kyron can grab them, for now, I'm sure she will bring some more later."

"Sure, tea or coffee?" Kyron asks.

"Tea please. Milk and, better make it 3 sugars. I might need it." He replies, gesturing for me to go ahead.

Kyron nods, and turns back towards the kitchenette I'd just left, but not before giving me an apologetic look. He knew I heard them and he was ashamed. So he should be! How dare he presume how much I could handle or what I should or shouldn't hear! I would hazard a guess that, if the tables were turned, he would be in the exact position I was right now. I shouldn't give it anymore thought though. I need to concentrate on Jack and Skye. What happens next could cause major repercussions on their marriage.

Troy and I enter the small conference room with the drinks, capturing Skye and Jack in a small embrace, it was a little one sided on Skye's part but she didn't seem to mind.

"Everything ok?" Troy asks with a smile.

"Yes thank you sir," Jack replies. "I'm deeply sorry for all that's happened."

Troy holds up his hand in a friendly stop motion. He then lets out a little, childlike giggle, much to my surprise.

"Let's not start just yet," he says. "Let's wait for everyone else to get here, that way; we don't have to go over everything multiple times."

"Of course, sorry, I wasn't thinking," Jack replies. "I just wanted to get it all out in the open."

"It's ok Jack, we understand but, please, take your time," I say gently. "There's no rush."

Jack lets out an audible sigh, not of relief but out of frustration. He starts to taps his fingers on the table and bob his leg up and down. If the others don't get here soon, I'm worried he won't help at all.

"How much longer Troy?" I ask,

"They should be here any minute, give or take." He replies, looking at his watch.

"Give or take what?" I say. "Its 11pm! There's no traffic holding them up!"

"Shea, relax. I can wait. I'm just feeling a little nervous, that's all." Jack says, quietly.

"Are you sure you're alright?" Skye asks him. "This is a big thing; don't you want to rest first?"

"No! I have to do this. I've lied too long now. It's time for the truth," he snaps.

Skye sits back startled. "I'm sorry," is all she can manage to say.

Chapter 29

Derek stops at the front door of his, once, giggly, family home. He and Harriet hadn't laughed properly since Jemma came back two years ago.

Harriet had always been busying herself, trying to stop Jemma drinking. She thought he didn't know, he knew. He knew more that he showed, he kept it all locked in his mind. He knew Harriet could control Jemma but when she started playing around with magic, it scared him. He was always taken back to the stories of when his grandmother was accused of being a witch. She was paraded through the town with a rope around her neck whilst people threw stones at her and spat at her. She suffered a heart attack in the street, no one helped her, his mother had told him all the details in intricate description, and he had dreamt about it so vividly.

He can hear Lenora's' voice from inside, then faintly Harriets'. The low voices and hushed laughter make him wish Jermaine were still here. He took a deep breath and turned the key. The smell of roast beef hit his nostrils like a wave hits the beach, washing over him with every sniff. Harriet hadn't cooked like this since Jemma returned from London. He missed this. This sense of home.

"I'm back," he says, trying to make his voice sound chirpy.

"Are you alright Derek?" Lenora asks.

"I think so," he replies. "Where's Harriet?"

"Taking a bath, what's up?" she asks. "Do you want to talk about it?"

"Would you mind?" he asks. "I'll put the kettle on."

Harriet can hear Derek downstairs, she hasn't realised how long he had been gone until she quickly checks the time on her watch. It has been 4 hours. Where had he been all this time? She lay back in the bath and let herself relax before she went back downstairs. She trusted her husband and also knew that he needed his own space from time to time, she could allow him that, especially since he had given her space to deal with Jemma's 'tantrums', at least that what he thought they were. She was so glad he didn't know what was happening; it would break him seeing Jemma like that. It's exactly how his mother had been the last time her saw her as she took her last breath.

"So, Derek, are you going to speak or shall I attempt to read your mind?" laughs Lenora.

"Sorry Len, I was daydreaming. I went to Jermaine's grave today. I laid some flowers and told him how brave Shea had been today. My heart burst with pride Len." He says whilst a solitary tear rolls down his ageing face.

"Oh Dez!" Lenora says, giving his arm a light pat. "Why didn't you say you were going? Harriet and I would have come with you."

"I needed to be alone, if you can understand that," he replies. "She did so well Len. I wish he had been here to see that."

"I understand fully, but what has got you so muffled?" she asks.

"I'm not sure if what I felt was pride or jealousy, I'm positive it was pride. I can't help but feel jealous that you still have Shea and that we've lost Jemma," he finishes.

"That is something I can definitely understand!" she says quietly. "I feel the same about Harriet still having you and Jermaine being taken from me. It's completely natural to have those feelings Dez; I take no offence at all."

Derek smiles, happy that they are all still on good terms despite their own setbacks.

"What have I missed?" Harriet says, kissing Derek on the forehead.

"I went to Jermaine's grave today," he repeats with a lopsided smile.

"Oh love, are you alright?" she replies with a sad face.

"I am now I'm home. Len, will you join us for dinner? It smells delicious," he says.

Lenora swipes at her face with the sleeve of her pale blue cardigan, "only if there is enough to go around," she smiles.

Harriet pulls her in for a hard hug, holding tight and taking a deep breath in.

"There's always enough for you Len," she says. "Always."

"So, do we call you Jack or Elijah?" The therapist asks.

She'd turned up, finally, 8 minutes late without an apology and had huffed her way through the briefing on exactly why she was here. I had to leave the room; I really wanted to spin her head on her shoulders to see if there was any life in there!

"Jack please, if you don't mind?" he says, looking at Skye as if seeing permission.

"Whatever you are comfortable with," Skye encourages him, squeezing his hand and giving him a smile.

"Ok Jack, let's start from the beginning." She says, sounding as bored as ever. I wondered if she was like this with all her clients or if it's just because it's gone 11pm. We will never know.

"Well, um, I met Saskia when we were very young, maybe 15, or 16. We started out as friends, laughing and joking around," he says smiling as he remembers the fun they both had.

Miss Snootyshirt writes everything down as he speaks, glancing up once or twice to encourage him to continue. I wish she would show him some compassion, he's basically telling his whole life story to a statue.

"We split up a few times before she fell pregnant with the girls. I was so happy. I promised her and the girls the world. They would want for nothing," he says as he turns to look at Skye. She gives him a reassuring smile that he takes as consent to continue. "Saskia had a really complicated pregnancy; she suffered with pre-eclampsia and really nasty morning sickness. I had to take her to the hospital so many times," he says, closing his eyes as a single tear escapes his eye.

I can see the pain in his face as he remembers those days. He looks up at me and I give him a solemn smile, one that meant I was here and I can help.

"Please continue when you're ready Jack," Miss Snootalot says gruffly. She is really putting me on edge.

Chapter 30

They didn't speak throughout their meal. All deep in their own thoughts.

"May I make a toast?" Harriet says, holding up her mug of tea high above her head.

"Of course dear, but what to?" Derek asks lightly.

"Not what, but who," she replies still grasping her mug over her head. "To those we have lost, friends, family pets and memories, we hold close those we still have and treasure the future of memories with will create," she says, giving Lenora's shoulder a gentle squeeze. "To Shea, Lenora, Derek and I. To Jermaine, Jemma, Fudge, and Spitfire!" Harriet ends with a smile and a giggle.

Lenora bursts out laughing at the mention of the girls' pet hamsters names. She remembers when she took them to collect the pets from the shop. How Shea came up with the Spitfire was beyond everyone, including Jermaine!

"That was lovely Harriet," Lenora says. "Thank you for allowing me to share your toast and your fabulous meal."

"You know you are more than a friend Len. You always have been and that will never change." She replies with a smile.

Derek collects the plates and washes then up while the two women settle in the living room. He makes one last cup of tea before retiring to bed, leaving Harriet to finish her chat with Lenora.

"She had the girls early, around 35-36 weeks. Vanessa first, then about 2 minutes later Annalise arrived. She was so blue, so abnormally blue," his voice trailing off as he remembers the birth of his daughters so vividly.

Miss Snootysnoots writes everything down then looks at him with a stare that could turn water to ice.

"They took her away so quickly, ran her to NICU. I followed behind, the nurse didn't notice me. I could hear them talking about a cord and lack of oxygen. She was put on to a machine to help her breathe properly. My little princess was so blue," he sobs.

Skye reaches for him but he pulls away, she flinches but doesn't complain, she understands.

"What next Jack?" I prompt him. "Did you see her again?"

He looks directly into my eyes. The sadness is so clear to anyone with a heart.

"No," he answers. Just one word sums up how badly he was affected by it all. "Saskia was cuddling and feeding Vanessa when I got back there. I couldn't tell her what I had just seen; it would break her in half, so I kept it to myself, planted a smile on my face, and held Vanessa for hours whilst Saskia slept."

He takes a deep breath, steadies himself, and stands up. He shoves his hands into pockets and walks towards the window. There isn't much to see out there, it backs on to the fields, which by now are as dark as the darkest void of space, but it seems to calm him down.

Chapter 31

"I wonder how they are getting on at the station," Lenora says, watching out the window as the world passed by without a second thought.

"I'm sure they will be finished soon and then Shea will be back home and you can stop wearing that patch any deeper on the carpet," Harriet laughs.

"I just worry about her," Lenora replies. "I'm sorry."

"Don't be sorry," Harriet says with a flick of her hand, "we both know it's perfectly normal."

The two women laughed. They were always worrying about the girls, especially when they were younger, spending endless hours in the woods, coming back looking like they had been digging for gold, they were always together.

Derek could hear them both laughing. It brought a smile to his face. He always enjoyed hearing them laugh. He and Jermaine would sometimes sit on the back step and listen to them, it brought them joy.

"Oh I wish you could see them Jay, just like the old days," he says, looking skywards.

Derek goes to the dresser and pulls out the old photo album. He opens the first page to the two smiling faces of Jemma and Shea, arms wrapped around each other like two sides of a comfort blanket. As he flips through the pages, endless amounts of memories come flooding back. From the time, Shea fell out of the tree, to the time Jemma tried to give the Evergreen tree a perm using her Mum's hair rollers. He didn't hear the door open behind him. He just sat there laughing between tears. Harriet gently touches his shoulder and he blindly pats her hand.

"I'll be alright love," he says, swiping at his eyes.

"I know you will. Would you mind joining us downstairs, there's something I need to tell Len and I would like you to be there too," she says softly, giving his hand a squeeze.

"What is it?" he asks, worryingly.

"Just come down and all will be revealed!" she says, trying to sound mysterious but just laughs instead.

"Ha Ha, alright, I will be right down," he laughs, getting up to put the album back in its place.

"Jack?" I ask, "Are you alright?"

"I don't really have an answer for that right now," he says, looking off into the distance. "I don't know if I ever will have or if I ever will be."

I'm no body language expert but he doesn't look comfortable at the moment.

"Will this take much longer?" Miss Snootyshirt asks.

"That's it!" I shout. "How seriously do you take your job?" I ask, mere inches from her face.

"I don't appreciate your tone Miss," she says with a roll of her eyes.

I swear I just want to shake her like a glow stick to see if the light comes on.

"Do you have ANY idea what we have ALL been through? Do you?" I say through gritted teeth. I haven't moved an inch and I will continue to stand my ground until she either does her job properly of I throttle her, whichever comes first.

"No Miss, that's why I was dragged from my bed, to come here and listen to this," she gestures to Jack standing at the window.

"JACK!" I say, nearly growling at her "has been through a lot!"

Snooty looks me up and down, rolls her eyes again, grabs her bag, notebook, herself, and leaves the room. I wish I could knock her eyes into the depths of her soul, if she has one.

"What the hell was that all about Shea?" Kyron shouts.

"She wasn't doing her job, that's what that was, and if you had been doing yours, you would have found someone better!" I yell back, still glued to the spot. I won't back down.

"Now what do we do? She was the only person available at such short notice." Troy adds, holding his head in his hands.

I take a deep breath, hold for 5 seconds, and breathe out slowly. Why was I so frustrated?

"Sorry, I know short hand if you need anything written up quickly," Skye offers in a small, mouse like voice.

"It's not procedure but it will do for now." Troy says, smiling at her.

I do believe she is truly an angel.

Chapter 32

Derek makes his way downstairs, all the while wondering what Harriet had to tell Len that was so important. He couldn't think of anything.

"Hurry up dear!" Harriet says from the bottom step. "This is a big thing and I'm not sure how long I will have the confidence."

Derek hadn't realised he had stopped 7 steps from the bottom.

"Sorry love, I'm coming," he says, mentally snapping himself back to reality.

Derek walks behind his wife of 54 years, ready to support her, no matter what.

"Len, come sit with me," Harriet says, patting the seat next to her on the sofa.

"What's wrong Harriet?" Len replies, instantly worried but taking the seat offered.

"I have something that I need to tell you. I've been wanting to say something for a few days now but so much has happened." Harriet says, trying not to hold out too long.

Lenora sat up straighter, looking at Harriet and then at Derek.

"Do you know anything about this?" She asks him, a little sterner that she intended.

"Not a dickie bird, I promise," he replies. "This will be news to be as much as you."

"Out with it!" Lenora snaps.

"Well, a while ago I was searching through my family history, mainly for Jemma. I traced some of my older family members who told me that I was, essentially, a twin, not identical." Harriet says, faster that she expected.

"You found your twin? Why would this be important to me?" Lenora asks. "Do you want me to be there when you finally meet him or her?"

"It's not that Len, in fact, I already have met her," Harriet says, looking down at her hands.

"When?" Derek demands. "You never leave the house!"

Derek then realises what Harriet means. He looks again at his wife and her best friend, sitting in almost the same manner, mirroring each other perfectly. He takes a deep breath.

"Derek, are you alright?" Lenora asks.

"Harriet, you need to get all of this out now. I'm not always the brightest bulb in the chandelier but if I'm correct with the conclusion I've come to, you need to tell her, and now." He says.

"Lenora, my oldest, dearest friend," Harriet says, taking her hands and giving it a gentle squeeze. "You are my twin! Didn't you ever wonder why our birthdays were on the same day?"

"I...I just put it down to coincidence..I never had any siblings growing up. I..I don't know if I can handle this right now," She replies. "I have to go home."

With that, she left.

Skye quickly wrote up everything that had already been discussed. She was very quick.

"Ready when you are," she says as she finishes the last word.

"Jack?" I ask. "You ready to continue, or do you need a break?"

"No, I need to do this but, could I have some water, please?" he replies.

"I'll go, ice?" Kyron says, clearly still annoyed with me. Tough!

"No, thank you," Jack replies quietly.

Kyron leaves the room, slamming the door behind him.

"Is he angry at me?" Jack asks, looking like a frightened little boy.

"No, no, he's angry with at me, don't worry," I say soothingly.

"He will calm down soon, he's not used to women standing up to him," Troy says with a giggle.

Jack smiles, just a small smile, but it's there. I watch as Skye follows his every move, pen poised to begin writing as soon as he starts talking.

"Saskia woke up early the next morning, crying out for Annalise. I held her whilst I tried to explain that they had taken her upstairs to be looked after, but she fought me off and demanded to see the doctor." Jack recalls, staring off over the darkened fields.

"Did they explain what had happened to her?" I ask, careful not to push him.

"They said she passed away over night, but didn't want to disturb Saskia. I was so angry. I grabbed him and threw him across the room," Jack says, now staring at his hands as if he still held the doctor.

"What happened to the doctor?" Troy asks, surprising us all. This is the first question he has asked since we all go back.

Jack turns to face him. "He broke both of his legs and shattered his pelvis. He will be in a wheelchair for the rest of his life. I'm not proud of what I did, please believe me?" Jack says, not flinching from his own honesty but pleading for forgiveness.

"I believe you," Kyron says from the doorway. "I was there."

We all turn to look at Kyron. No one says a word.

Chapter 33

"How long have you known?" Derek demands.

"Only a few months, honestly, I didn't fully believe it myself," Harriet replies. "Then I was sent this photo." Harriet shows Derek the photo sent to her from her elderly family member. It shows 2 babies side by side in an incubator. The names read 'Harriet' and 'Lindsay'.

"How can you even be sure that Len is Lindsay?" He asks. "There is no definitive way you could tell from that picture!"

"But there is! Look closer," she replies. She points out the odd shape of Lindsay's' ear. "Len's ear is exactly the same!" she says as she points it out in one of the photos from the album Derek was browsing through earlier.

"It does seem awfully similar," Derek admits, looking closer. He had to admit; they were very close and seemed to share similar interests.

"Did this family member give you any more information, like why you weren't brought up together?" Derek asks, still puzzled over the whole thing.

"They said Mum could only afford to keep one of us, and with me looking the most 'normal', they chose to have Len adopted," she replies, using her fingers to accentuate the word normal.

"Didn't you think about how this would affect Len?" he says, rubbing the back of his neck.

"Honestly Derek! I've just found my twin sister and you expect me to think of someone else's feelings? This is the first time I can really smile since Jemma!" she shouts.

Derek was speechless. Never in the 54 years of marriage and 56 years together has he ever seen his wife act so selfish. He didn't say another word. He turned his back on her for the first time ever, and walked up the stairs, went to the bathroom and there he remained until he could remember who his wife was before all this. Harriet sat in the same place on the sofa sobbing. She couldn't understand why she should have thought of anyone else but herself. This was a big thing for her to find out. 'No one understood that' she told herself.

Everyone was staring at Kyron like he had just spoken after years of being mute. No one had even heard him come back in.

"What did you say?" I ask quietly.

"I was there," he replies. "I wasn't always a cop. I studied paediatric medicine."

This was news to everyone in the room. Skye was still watching Jack, his face showing a little sign of recognition. Just a little.

"The question everyone is scared to ask here is; why didn't you recognise him when you first saw him?" Troy asks.

He was right. Everyone turns to look at him, their faces showing the same expressions. That was the burning question.

"He changed his appearance, at least that's what everyone thought, but looking at him now, I can see that he has just aged a lot and is using colour contacts for his eyes." Kyron

responds. We all understood why he did what he did, even the doctor, hence why he didn't press charges."

I'm dumbfounded. The whole time Kyron has ultimately been friends with this guy, he hasn't even figured who he really was. He knew Jacks background but didn't disclose anything. Why? I mean, it would explain all the sightings leading to nothing, because he was here all along, in some ways, trying to move on with his life.

"Sorry to break your train of thought Shea, but can I speak about the night with Jemma?" Jack says quietly. "I think you need to hear this more than the rest, if you don't mind?"

"Erm, yes, of course, sorry. I was just thrown off a bit there. If you're' sure you're ready?" I reply.

He nods, takes his place at the table, and gestures for me to sit to the left of him, with Skye to his right. Kyron places himself next to Skye and Troy brings up his chair closer to my side. He gently pats my shoulder as a sign that he is there if I need him. I may just need someone. I wish you were here Dad; please give me some strength to get through this night.

Derek taps on the window, in the same way he used to knock before, just so she knows it's him.

"I'm so sorry Len," he says. "I honestly had no idea."

"It's ok. I'm just so stunned that she could just come out with it like nothing else was important anymore!" she says with tears in her eyes.

Derek really didn't know what to say. He couldn't even defend his wife because he felt the same as Lenora.

"I'm sorry," she says as she runs off to the bathroom.

Derek sits there with his head in his hands. Why had Harriet chosen now to say something? What had happened to his one considerate wife?

"Don't take it to heart Dez."

Derek jumps up and spins round. There stands Zephyr.

"I don't know what to say to her Jay!" Derek says quietly, "I don't want their friendship ruined by this."

"I know, it's hard. I think there's a long path ahead for them both, you'll need to be strong for them all," he replies.

"Who are you talking to Derek?" Len says as she enters the room and glimpses the stark red hair.

"Erm, Len, this is.." Derek starts.

"Hi bumpkin." Zephyr finishes.

Lenora grasps the chair and sobs so hard. Derek guides her to the Jermaine's old chair, goes to switch the kettle on, and calls Harriet. She started this whole thing. She can see it through to the end and see the outcome.

Chapter 34

Jack takes a deep breath, this is going to be hard on both of us, but in order to help him, I have to know everything, even if I really don't want to hear it.

"I had seen Jemma a few times around town, when I was out with Skye. I knew who she was and I knew she would recognise me, so I kept my distance. Jemma was a clever girl. I saw her in the club, in the pub and in the shops buying alcohol. I even tried to stop her once, told her it wouldn't fix or solve anything," he says, staring straight ahead, not wanting to look anyone in the eye for fear it would put him off what he needed to say.

"I remember that time," Skye says softly. "You tried so hard, but she just snatched the bottle and ran away."

I turn to Skye and smile. "That sounds just like her, stubborn!"

"Take your time Jack, we have plenty of time left," Troy says with a smile that could melt ice.

Jack smiled back, just a little, with no eye contact.

"She brushed me off with some story about ruining her career and nearing the end of her friendship with her best friend," he says, looking at me. "I knew she meant you."

"Why the letters Jack?" I ask. I needed to know why. If he wanted to help her, why threaten her.

"They were drunken mistakes and shouldn't have happened, so please Chief Inspector Lysine, add those charges too," he says looking at Troy.

"Please call me Troy," he responds.

Jack nods in agreement.

"I followed her home one night, a night when I had built up enough courage to venture out alone. Skye was on a late and I knew she wouldn't be home for hours. I wanted to ask her to help me; she was a solicitor after all, wasn't she supposed to help people? I could hear her shouting for Shea, so I climbed the trellis next to her window and climbed in, I could see she was sleeping but she was thrashing about, a lot. I tried to wake her up; she pulled a hunting knife from under her pillow and blindly swung it around. I kept dodging it," he says closing his eyes as the tears fall. "I grabbed her wrist, tried to get the knife from her but she kept struggling against me, she tried to push me away but she slipped and the knife..." he stops, as the sobs got deeper and louder, but they weren't from him, they were from me.

The kettle clicks off in the silence; no one had uttered a word. Derek busied himself making tea for Harriet and Lenora, the whole time trying to work out how to explain who Zephyr really was. He loads up the tea tray and carries it through to the living room.

Lenora hasn't moved from the chair Derek sat her in not more than 5 minutes ago, but she also hasn't taken her eyes on Zephyr. Harriet is silent for a change, eyeing between Lenora, Derek, and Zephyr.

"Who is he?" she asks, gesturing to Zephyr. "He doesn't look normal."

Derek gives his wife a cup of tea and a biscuit, hoping it will keep her quiet for at least 10 minutes. He kneels next to Lenora and hands her a cup, she looks at him in the eyes but says nothing, her eyes say it all. Derek slowly bows his head but remains silent. This is Zephyrs show now.

"Explain." Is the only word Lenora speaks.

"It's me bumpkin. It's Jay. It's too hard to explain fully right now, I could vanish at any time to be there for Shea," he starts.

"She knows about you?" she interrupts.

"Not who I really am," he says holding his palms up. "She knows me as Zephyr; a spirit who protects her in her dreams. Jemma learnt some form of magic before passing over. She arranged for me to take this on. To protect and guide our daughter," he finishes.

"Jemma?" Harriet shouts almost dropping her tea and biscuit. "How dare you speak of her?"

"Harriet! It's Jay! He wouldn't harm her!" Derek interrupts her barrage of abuse.

"I'm confused," Lenora says a little quieter this time. "How can I be so sure it is you?"

"If I wasn't me, would I know that your favourite colour is pastel orange and that you prefer 100% cotton sheets as opposed to Egyptian cotton?" he replies with a smile. "Sadly we don't get to choose our appearance when doing this," he says chuckling as he catches a glimpse of himself in the mirror above the fireplace.

Lenora laughed through tears. She was so happy to see him again, even if he did look like a circus clown! She stood up, opened her arms, and hugged him tight.

"Shea will be so thrilled to see you!" she whispered in his ear.

"No, we can't tell her!" he says back.

"Why not?" Harriet exclaims. "She has a right to know!"

"She does, but if she knows who I really am, I will not be able to return to her, I need to be there for her." He replies. "Please, for her sake if nothing else, I've longed for the days to watch her live a long life."

"She won't say a word. That's a promise," Derek says, shaking his hand.

"Thank you, you're a true friend," he says with a tear.

Chapter 35

I pull myself together enough to face the people in the room. I must look a mess.

"So, she slipped?" Kyron asks.

"Yes, she tried to push me away and she slipped on the silk sheets on her bed. I tried to stop her but she slipped and fell on the knife. It went through her chin and up into her mouth. There was so much blood. I'm not good with blood," Jack turns to look at Skye who is still writing everything down.

"Those stupid sheets! I told her to get rid of them ages ago! They go all static and make her hair stand up on end." I say quietly.

Troy touches my hand lightly, I look up and smile. "Thanks." I can just about manage to say.

He says nothing back, just dips his head. He and Dad go on so well and respected each other. I hope I can gain that same respect one day.

"What happened next?" I ask, I don't want to know but in order to help him, I have to know everything.

"There was blood everywhere, it was just gushing from her neck!" he says, his face losing all of its colour. "I ran!"

"You did WHAT?" I scream.

I promised myself I wouldn't lose my temper. I lied!

I couldn't believe he would just run, I mean, no one really likes blood do they? He could have tried to help stop the bleeding. He could have called for the ambulance; he didn't even have to give his details, just an address.

"I'm sorry Shea," he says sounding like a toddler who has just dropped a prize piece of china.

"I can't believe you just left her!" I say, trying not to let my emotions get the better of me.

"When I found out she had died, I couldn't sleep, I couldn't eat, I couldn't even look Skye in the eyes," he says, looking at Skye once more.

"I remember. You said you weren't feeling well so I just left you to rest in bed," she says quietly.

"Why aren't you angry with me Skye?" he asks softly.

"I don't know. I'm not sure if I should be angry, more disappointed, and sad that you didn't trust me enough to ask for my help," she says without looking at him.

This must be hard for her, without having to take notes too. She is still coming to terms with the fact her husband isn't who he said he was, she's strong, I'll give her that!

"Why did you keep following me? What happened with Sierra? I ask.

He breaks down crying. Just sits there crying, he doesn't even try to hide it. He just lets the tears fall, like he doesn't care what anyone thinks.

Lenora and Harriet sit in silence at the kitchen table unsure of what to say to each other. For the first time in years, they were unable to speak to each other. They steal glances back and forth until Lenora finally gives up.

"This is ridiculous. We've known each other far too long for this to divide us," she says grabbing Shea's laptop and opening the internet browser.

She types 'DNA TESTING' into the search field. Within seconds, there are literally thousands of results. She takes her time reading reviews and rating of each one and finally settles on the fifth result, with a 24-hour turnaround time and results emailed to them. She ordered the tests to arrive the next day via courier, he would then wait, and courier them back to the lab.

"Time we found out for certain!" she says when she has finished. "Remember, you don't have to be blood to be family!"

Harriet is speechless; she let the tears fall without shame. For the first time ever, Harriet had absolutely nothing to say, no comebacks, or quirky remarks. Nothing could change their friendship, it was too strong. They had brought their children up together, gone on holidays as one big family, enjoyed Christmases together; there wasn't an event they hadn't shared together. Bound by friendship.

"You two are joint at the hip, just like our girls were," Derek says, breaking the silence. He grabs Harriets hand, "Zephyr will take care of Jemma."

"You mean Jay," laughs Lenora.

Harriet just smiles. She doesn't even attempt to speak; She knew she would just cry so she just squeezes his hand.

"Now," Lenora says loudly, making them both jump. "Who wants tea? I can't sleep knowing Shea is still there with him."

"I'll...I'll give you a hand." Harriet manages with a smile.

Derek watches them in the kitchen, acting as if the last few hours hadn't happened, linked together with an unbreakable bond. He watches them laugh, joke and smile whilst making the tea, laying out a variety of biscuits and slices of cakes onto a tray. Lenora always laid out cake with her tea, for as long as he could remember. Jermaine said she should have run a teashop! Derek giggled to himself as he remembered. Maybe she still could, they could do it together, he thought to himself. Something to look in to later. They bring the tray through to the living room, sit down, and start to pour the tea. This sight makes Derek smile. No fights, no drama, as if none of this had ever happened. The shrill of the phone makes them all jump. They all look at each other with concern. Lenora stands up, straightens her cardigan, and picks up the receiver.

"Hello, Hopewell residence?" she says.

"Mum, it's me." I say when she finally answers the phone. "What took you so long? Did I wake you?"

"Oh Shea darling! No, no, I can't sleep until you're back here safely," Lenora replies, tears pricking at her eyes.

"Mum, you really need to rest," I tell her instantly feeling guilty that she is still awake waiting for me. "I'll be back soon. We have nearly finished here, but Mum, it's been hard."

"You're a stronger person than I am darling. We have had an eventful evening here too, but that can wait until you get back. I love you." She replies before hanging up.

I stand there for a moment holding the phone before Troy gently shakes me from my thoughts.

"Everything alright at home?" he asks.

"That's a really good question but I'm not sure. She said it's been eventful but then she hung up!" I reply, still trying to work out what she meant.

Troy just giggles to himself. "She always was cryptic!" he says, still laughing. "Try not to worry too much. We're nearly done here, and then you can go home and find out what's been so eventful!"

"Let's get this done then!" I say, giving every effort I can to smile.

I walk back towards the conference room still wondering what Mum had meant. I could hear raised voices coming from inside. Try had already gone in when I approached the doorway. I was stunned to see, that what I instinctively thought was commotion, was in fact Kyron, Jack and Skye joking about the most recent episode of popular soap opera. I let out a deep sigh of relief I didn't realise I was holding.

"I can hear you three from down the corridor!" I say, trying to make my voice strong, but then laughing along with them.

"Sorry Shea," laughs Skye. "Kyron does an awesome impression of Tyler from Best Mates!"

"Oh please! Don't show me!" I say, holding my hands up. "I hate him."

Jack looks different whilst he is laughing. Almost as if he is at peace with things, but we still have things to talk about. I clear my throat.

"Shall we continue? The sooner we get this done, the sooner we can look into getting contact with Vanessa." I say quietly.

Jack nods with determination. "Let's get it done!" he says.

I smile at him, then at Skye. She looks a little more relaxed than before; maybe everyone just needed a break.

Skye settled herself in a comfortable position; pen in hand ready to write. I know I'll still worry about her after this, but she is a strong woman.

"So Jack," Troy starts, "What happened with Sierra?"

Jack takes a deep breath, closes his eyes, and begins to talk.

"She looked so much like you Shea," he says, his eyes still closed. "I didn't mean for her to die. She was fighting back when I was holding her arms. She was shouting at me, telling me she wasn't Shea and that her name was Sierra. I didn't believe her. I said I only wanted to talk but she was fighting me. I slammed her against the wall and she hit her head, she just slumped down to the ground so I ran, again. I assumed someone would find her and get help. I was so angry with myself when she died. That's why I did what I did to you and Skye," he says, opening his eyes and looking straight into my eyes.

"That was your cry for help?" Kyron asks quietly.

"Yes. That's when I realised I needed help. I needed to tell someone but I've never known how. Only how to do bad things, Mum said I was good at being bad. I thought that was a good thing, now I know it isn't." He says, looking towards Kyron. "I am truly sorry and would like to try and write a letter to her parents to convey my remorse."

"We will work on that too Jack, don't worry." I say, sitting down on his left side. He turns to face me.

"I'm sorry if I scared your Mum, she seems like a really nice lady," he says, looking down at his hands.

"She is, but she's going through a tough time at the moment and all this has been too much for her," I reply, trying not to sound annoyed with him, it's not like he knows she has cancer.

Lenora looks at the clock. It's gone 2am and no sign of Shea. She starts to worry again and begins to pace the kitchen. Harriet and Derek have drifted off to sleep on the sofa; she has changed into her pyjamas and wrapped herself in Jermaine's old dressing gown for comfort. She inhales the fading scent of his aftershave. She always feels safe when she can smell him. She smiles on the inside, settles herself in to the recliner chair in the corner of the room, and slowly drifts off to sleep. She jumps up a few hours later to the sound of voices in the kitchen. She notices that Derek and Harriet have gone so she gathers herself together and makes her way to the kitchen. To her relief, there stands Shea, all radiance and smiles. She stands between Harriet and Derek, seeing this makes Lenora's heart skip a beat. Her baby girl is home safe.

Chapter 36

"So that's it?" Mum asks, "He just waits for a trial date?"

"Yes Mum. Troy and Kyron will find a way for him to have some form of contact with Vanessa whilst he waits for trial and hopefully while he is in prison," I reply.

I had told them all what had happened to Jack and handed Derek and Harriet a letter that Troy had helped Jack write to them. They had cried whilst they read it together. I've not a clue what was written. I promised Jack I wouldn't read it or ask what it said, and I intend to keep that promise, that is between him and them.

Troy had taken Jack to a secure unit where he will have a professional psych assessment and get some help if he needs it. Skye has been advised to see a therapist to help her come to terms with what has happened. She has vowed to stand by Jack no matter what, which makes her a stronger woman than me by a long shot!

Harriet and Derek leave around 6am, clutching the letter from Jack. I couldn't tell anyone what was said in that room, but they would find out from the trial. I make Mum a hot water bottle and settle her into bed for a while. She needs the rest and she looked shattered. I make my way to my old room and I am stunned by the state of it! I don't have the energy to tidy it now. I collapse on the bed and let sleep claim me without even undressing. I have a lot on my mind but I need to fully recharge for me to be able to deal with it all.

'I'm back in the woods again but this time it's different. The sun is beating down on me, the daffodils and daises are in full bloom. There's no shouting, no footsteps besides my own. Then I see him.

"So, back again I see!" Zephyr says with a wide grin. "I thought I'd seen the back of you."

"I never thought I'd see you again," I say, pulling him in for a hug. "Thank you. You helped me so much."

"Just doing what was asked of me," he shrugs.

"Well still, thank you." I say. "I miss Jemma."

"I know. She misses you too. Just remember, she will always be with you," he says, waving. "I'll see you soon!"

Then he was gone.

I wake up after a few hours to the sound of a phone ringing. I realise it's actually my phone ringing. I look at the caller ID.

'TROY'

I wonder why he is calling.

"Hello?" I say, trying not to sound too groggy.

"Hi Shea, sorry to call you this early. I know it's barely 9:30am and you've probably not had much sleep, but we've been given a preliminary hearing date for Friday. Will you still be able to attend? I know you are due back in London on Wednesday afternoon," he rushes to say.

"Of course. I will have my case handed over to one of the senior staff at the office. I won't break a promise," I reply, making a note to call my boss later on. "Any luck with Vanessa?"

"Not as yet, but we're working on it," he replies. "Get some more sleep. I'll drop by in a few hours."

With that, he hung up. I sit up some more and stretch until my back cracks; I must have fallen asleep in an awkward position. I decide to quickly check on Mum; she normally gets up early no matter how late she sleeps. I peek into her room and see that she is still sleeping peacefully with a smile on her face. She's finally relaxed. I slowly close the door and go back to my room. I don't think I can go back to sleep, so I tackle the mess that's been left in here. I'll have to ask Mum what on Earth happened in here.

I could hear voices downstairs piercing my ears. Realising I fell asleep on the pile of clothes near the wardrobe; I force myself to stand, grab a shower, and go down to the noise. I can instantly recognise Harriet, Troy and Derek, as well as Mum, but there was another voice I hadn't heard before.

I enter the room smiling with an ease I hadn't felt in a while.

"Ah Shea! It's so nice to see you smiling again sweetheart!"

Harriet beams, she sounds a lot happier than before.

"Hi Harriet, Derek, Troy. Morning Mum," I say as I kiss her on the forehead.

"Shea, this is Petra. She is with Children's Services." Troy introduces us. "Petra, this is Shea, she is handling Jacks case."

" Good morning Shea, I understand it has been an eventful period for you. I am truly sorry to hear about your friend. I am here to inform you that Vanessa was adopted just over 6 months ago. Saskia unfortunately passed away about 9 months ago." Petra says politely.

"Thank you Petra. I'm sorry to hear about Saskia. I hope Vanessa is with a good family now. I trust Troy has shown you all the details we took from Jack last night. How would contact be initiated?" I ask, smiling.

"She is with a lovely family now and progressing well through school. She's 9 now. After her Mum dies, we found some old diaries that back up everything Jack said. We are working with the family to initiate contact. I cannot promise anything as yet." Petra replies.

"That's all I can ask for, thank you." I reply, still smiling.

We chat for a while longer, the Troy excuse himself and Petra to fill in some paperwork and visit Jack at the unit. After they had gone, it suddenly dawned on me that I hadn't asked Mum about last night and the 'eventful' time.

"Mum, what happened last night that was so eventful?" I ask.

She looks at Harriet, then Derek, then back at me.

"Well darling..." she begins.

'DING DONG'

"It's here!" she says, going to answer the door. "Stay here and I'll explain everything."

Chapter 37

"What!" I shriek. "Are you sure?"

"Well, no, not yet. That why I ordered this," Mum says, pointing to the DNA test on the table.

Harriet and Mum had explained the whole situation to me and I had no words to explain how this made me feel. The woman I had grown up around could actually be my true blood auntie!

"How did you find out?" I finally ask.

"I was doing some research online and an old relative recognised your Mum in the photos I put up." Harriet answers, somewhat dismissively.

"Mum, you know nothing will change between you both, even if you're not related, you do everything together," I tell her,

"I have to know love," she replies squeezing my hands gently. "Are you ready Harriet?"

Harriet holds up her swab like a sword ready to do battle. I give them both a huge hug and go to find Derek.

"Derek, are you OK?" I ask, finding him in the garden next to the tree we planted for Dad.

"I'm fine Shea. Just remembering a few things about your Dad," he says, turning to look at me. "You remind me so much of him, I'm proud of you."

I hug him hard. I can't remember a time when he hasn't been there for me since Dad died.

Troy puts the receiver down after finishing the conversation with his wife. He finishes filling in the paperwork for the court case. Jack had been diagnosed with a multitude of mental health problems and he was now getting the help he so desperately needed all these years. Troy should inform Shea but he had felt a little tension between Mrs Hopewell and Mrs Summers, so he would leave it for today. He picks up the phone and dials a number he knows well. He listens to it ring; he is lost in the sound when he hears the voice.

"Hello Sir,"

"Skye, how are you doing?" he asks.

"Not too bad, but not fantastic either. I wish this was all a dream," she replies. "Has there been any news?"

Troy updates her on the outcomes of Jacks' assessments; he reassures her that he is getting all the help he needs. He tells her when the preliminary hearing and updates her on the details surrounding Vanessa. He can hear her silently sobbing and wishes he could do more for her but he can't change anything that has and will happen. He says his goodbyes and replaces the handset. He sits for a few moments in silence before a knock at the door breaks it.

"Come in," he says.

Kyron opens the door slightly.

"Sorry to disturb you Sir, but Petra from Children's Services is here. She has guests," he says quietly.

"Show them to the conference room. I'll be there in just a second." He replies.

Kyron nods quickly and closes the door. Troy is unsure who she has brought with her but is keen to find out. He stands, straightens his shirt, pulls on his jacket, and makes his way to the room.

Derek and I go back to Mum and Harriet.

"How long before the results come through?" I ask Mum.

"24 hours sweetheart," she replies.

I look between Mum and Harriet, I can see a slight resemblance, but I wish this hadn't happened now.

"We are going to head home now," Derek says, grabbing Harriets hand and pulling her to her feet. "I think you both need to rest some more."

"Don't forget to call me when they come through!" Harriet calls, as she is lead away.

Something isn't right here. Derek has never dragged Harriet away like that before. I sit Mum down and find out exactly what happened. Mum doesn't hold back, she tells me everything. I am shocked, I've never know Harriet to be so selfish. Couldn't she see what Mum was already going through?

"Do you want some tea?" Mum asks.

"Yes, why not," I reply cheerfully.

As she walks into the kitchen, my phone begins to ring. I pull it from my pocket and check the caller ID.

'TROY'

"Hello Troy, what's up?" I answer.

"Petra has just introduced me to Vanessa. She wants to meet you," he replies, bypassing any pleasantries.

"Erm, sure. I can be there in 10 minute, if it helps?" I reply.

"Great, I'll get Kyron to meet you out front," he says, and

then he hangs up.

Chapter 38

Kyron is pacing outside the police station when I turn the corner.

"Hey! What's up?" I ask.

"Oh hey, nothing's wrong, I can just never stand still," he replies cheerfully.

"OK, so where is she and why does she want to see me?" I ask, still a little unsure.

"That's the million dollar question!" he says, raising his eyebrows high like a crazy clown.

I laugh and follow him through the station; everything seems less crazy than it did before. Kyron shows me to the conference room we used just the night before. A room I really didn't want to come back to so soon. I take a deep breath and open the door. I see the young girl first, with her long dark brown hair tied up with a blue ribbon; she has the most amazing bright blue eyes that sparkle when the light hits them. She is dressed smartly with a hint of casual in dark blue jeans, a white t-shirt with a pink butterfly emblazoned on the front and a white cardigan. She looks older than her 9 years but her eyes look lost.

"Vanessa, this is Shea." Petra says to her.

"Hi Vanessa. It's lovely to meet you," I say, taking the chair two seats away from her. I don't want her to feel overcrowded in such a small space.

"Hello," she replies quietly. "Thank you for helping my Dad."

"You're more than welcome sweetie," I say trying not to cry.

This poor girl has been through so much already.

"We have told her everything," says a dark haired woman sitting to her right. "I'm Linda. My husband, Shaun, and I adopted Vanessa."

"It's lovely to meet you both," I say, looking from her to him.

They both smile at Vanessa and me. We talk for a while longer about how much Vanessa understands about the current situation and answer all of her questions.

"When can I see him?" she asks.

I look at Troy and he excuses himself.

"I think it could be soon, but I can't promise anything just yet. Your Dad is somewhere safe, where people are helping him get better," I say.

She looks up at Kyron, who pulls a funny face at her; he'll be a great Dad one day. She tries to smile but it doesn't quite reach her eyes. I reach across the table to take her hand, but she reaches for mine and squeezes tight. My heart breaks for this poor girl.

Troy comes back in and slips his phone back into his pocket. Vanessa looks hopefully at him as if his next words will determine the rest of her life.

"The hospital says she can visit for one hour today. They are waiting for you now," he says to Linda and Shaun.

Vanessa jumps up and hugs him hard. He lets a single tear fall from his eye. I smile as he looks at me; I know he had to pull a few strings to arrange this. I'm positive this will help with Jack's recovery. We say our goodbyes and I wave her off to see her Dad for the first time in years. I hope this will be as good for you as it will be for him.

Lenora busies herself preparing dinner; she dices onions, carrots, and potatoes while the beef slowly cooks in the oven. She listens to her favourite songs and sings along with them all. During a gap in the playlist, she hears Shea laptop make a noise; she dries her hands and goes to look. Opening up the lid, she notices she left her own email open, and there is a new email highlighted, subject title DNA RESULTS. *That was a quick turnaround* she thought to herself, maybe they didn't have many to get through, and the lab is only 5 miles away. She decides not to open it yet, she can't do it alone. She goes back to her vegetables and continues to prepare for dinner. It has to be special; she decides to invite Harriet and Derek too. They should be here when she reads the results, this affects us all. Lenora feels a tickle in her throat so she coughs to clear it away but when she removes her hand from her mouth, she notices the blood, without a second thought, she quickly washes her hands and washes the blood away, *nothing to worry about, probably scratched my throat earlier with the crisps,* she thinks to herself. She can hear the front door open and close behind her.

"Mum, I'm home!"

I sniff the air and I know exactly what Mum is cooking, my stomach growls.

"Smells delicious Mum," I say, walking into the kitchen.

"You always say that," she replies, with a slightly nervous laugh.

"Everything alright Mum?" I ask, noticing how she laughs.

"Of course it is, you silly moo!" Mum says, laughing again. "I just got the results through my email; I hope you don't mind that I used your laptop. I'm going to invite Harriet and Derek for dinner then read them out. I haven't looked yet."

"Of course I don't mind Mum," I say. "I'll go wash up and get changed."

I smile at her; I can see how important this is to her. I quickly help lay the table, then go change, and call Harriet. I can hear Mum coughing in the kitchen so I make a mental note to get her to the doctors soon. I go into my room and look for something nice to wear. I should make an effort; this is a big night for Mum.

"I pick the blue jumpsuit!"

I cover my scream before Mum hears me.

"Zephyr! What are you doing here?" I ask, closing the door quickly.

"Did you not listen to a word I said to you that day," he says, shaking his head and giggling. "You know why I appear!"

"I did listen, yes, but I'm not scared here, I'm at home." I say confidently.

"Hmm, you give of a different vibe from confident, that's coming from deeper below the surface," he says, looking out of the window. "What's eating at you?"

"I'm worried about Mum, she has stage 3 breast cancer, has just found out her best friend could be her twin sister and her daughter was kidnapped," I say hysterically.

He stares at me with his mouth wide open.

"Cancer?" he asks.

"Yes, I'm terrified for her, I've already lost my Dad, that hurt like hell, I don't think I would survive if I lost her too," I say, trying not to cry.

"Your mother is a strong woman, I'm sure she will be fine," he says sounding hurt. "I will watch over you both, somehow." Then he is gone. How strange!

I use a face wipe to freshen up my face quickly, just so it doesn't look like I've been crying, or almost crying. I put the blue jumpsuit on, just as he suggested. Dad loved this colour.

Chapter 39

Jack and Vanessa have a tense hour together, getting to know each other again, but there is still a lot to explain that an hour won't allow. Linda and Shaun allow Vanessa to visit him alone, but they watch through the window. They sense he won't cause her any harm.

"I can see he's hurting," Shaun says, pulling his wife closer.

"We have to make sure she stays in contact with him. She has to understand everything about her life, it would be selfish of us not to," Linda replies, hugging him tight.

When their hour is over, Vanessa tentatively hugs him goodbye and promises to write to him as often as she can.

"Don't let your studies slip though. I want you to study hard, make everyone proud," Jack says to her.

She smiles and waves to him. Troy watches as they says goodbye, he notices a tear fall from Jack's eye. He understands how he feels, he can't imagine being apart from his children for any length of time other than work. Troy accompanies them to the exit and watches as they drive away, Vanessa looking out of the back window with sadness in her eyes. *That girl understands more than we give her credit for* he thinks. Troy goes back in to the hospital to get all the notes from Jack's nurse. He will let Shea know how things went later. This could really help Jack's case.

From my room, I can hear the doorbell ring.

"I'll get it!" Mum shouts as I walk down the stairs. "Oh my Shea! You look beautiful!"

"Oh Mum, stop it!" I say shyly. "It's an old jumpsuit, that I'm surprised still fits!"

"Was your Dad's favourite colour," she says, opening the door and welcoming Harriet and Derek.

"Hello Shea sweetheart," Derek says with a smile. "Doesn't seem 5 minutes since we were here last! How are you doing?"

"I'm well Derek thank you," I say, trying not to laugh. He's not wrong though, it seems they've spent a lot of time here this past few days, they might move in when I'm back in London! "How are you doing?"

"I'm holding up, hour by hour," he replies, turning to Harriet. "Her, minute by minute."

I let out a little giggle, Derek will never change, always a joke even at serious times.

"Shall we get dinner started?" Mum says, clapping her hands like a toddler waiting to open their Christmas presents.

We all laugh and make our way to the dining room, where Mum has laid out everything buffet style.

"It looks fabulous Len," Harriet says, taking a seat at the table.

Mum watches as we all sit down and begin to fill our plates. I look over to see her smiling off into the distance; I remember she hasn't laid the table like since our last Christmas with Dad. She catches me watching her and smiles at me. She gets up and heads to the living room where my laptop is, I know what she is doing, but I don't let on. I take a bite of the beef that just melts in my mouth, exactly how Mum has made it countless times before. Mum comes back with my laptop in her hands.

"I received an email earlier today," she announces. "It's the results. I've not checked it. Will you do it Harriet?"

Harriet looks between Mum, Derek and me. She points to me.

"Let Shea read it," she says.

I take a deep breath and look at Mum; she nods and passes me the laptop. Derek shifts his chair closer to mine.

"We'll look together," he says with a wink that transports me straight back to my childhood. He and Dad did that to us girls all the time.

I click on the email, Derek and I read it together. We exchange glances but not visible enough for either woman to catch us.

"What does it say darling?" Mum asks.

'Dear Mrs Hopewell,

We have examined both samples sent to us and have concluded the following result.

MRS LENORA HOPEWELL

MRS HARRIET SUMMERS

Share a 98% DNA match.

By these findings, it would be safe to assume that you are related.

I hope this is the news that you have been hoping for.

Sincerely

Jenny Hawkins.

Head of DNA Testing'

Everyone is silent, no one dares to speak.

"Mum?" I squeak, hardly recognising my own voice.

"I knew it! As soon as I was told, I knew it had to be you!" Harriet screeches. "I just knew it!"

"Harriet, sit down and shut up!" Derek says with authority. "Can't you see she is still in shock?"

Harriet looks hurt but sits down slowly, she looks at Mum.

"Aren't you happy?" she asks.

"I'm not sure yet. I have lived my whole life believing I was an only child, it's just so much to take in straight away," Mum replies sounding distant.

Harriet looks disappointed, she gets up and leaves.

"I'm sorry Len," Derek says, lightly squeezing Mums shoulder. He turns to me and attempts a smile, then follows his wife.

"I'm going for a lie down darling, I'll wash up later," Mum says, struggling to stand up.

I get up to help her but she shrugs me away with a smile. I wait until I hear her door close before breathing again.

"What can I do Dad?" I say to the now empty room. "I really wish you were still here."

I start to clear the plates away, I can hear Mum trying to cover up her coughing and the crying. My heart just breaks in two knowing that this is something I can't fix.

Chapter 40

Friday comes around quicker than I expect. Here I am, standing in my childhood bedroom, getting ready to attend court. I double-check I have everything before heading down for some breakfast. I have heard Mum pacing around the past few nights since the results came through, but I daren't ask her what's wrong, she will just give me some sill excuse and tell me to be on my way. That's how Mum is, never allows anyone to feel sorry for her. I can smell the bacon as soon as I open my bedroom door, Mum has always loved making breakfast, she says it sets you up for the day and stops your tummy rumbling until at least lunchtime! Who am I to argue with that?

I head downstairs where I can hear multiple voices, Mum, Harriet, Derek, but then there is a smaller voice, one I can just about hear if I strain hard enough. Harriet and Mum had spoken the day after the results came through. They decided not to let the results ruin what they have together and that they can now build more memories. I open the door to the dining room and see Petra, Troy, and Kyron.

"To what do I owe the pleasure of great company this morning?" I say as I smile at Vanessa's beautiful face, hidden behind a piece of toast.

She laughs behind it, which makes me smile. I look at Mum, who has a look of longing and sympathy in her eyes, but she looks so pale and tired, maybe I'll ask Harriet to stay here with her, or maybe I could ask the court to postpone until after I've had her checked out. I know Mum wouldn't allow me to do that.

"We thought we would escort you to the courtroom," Kyron says, attempting a posh voice but failing miserably.

I laugh at him, which in turn makes everyone else laugh.

I'd be grateful for a lift, ta," I say, letting my true Yorkshire accent shine through proudly. "Harriet, would you mind staying here with Mum today, she doesn't look herself."

"I'll keep an eye on her lovely, don't worry yourself," she replies with a smile, holding my hands tight.

I haven't managed to call her Aunt Harriet yet, I'm not sure if I ever will be ready for that, but she understands.

"Thank you," I manage to whisper.

We enter the court at the side entrance. I'm led straight to where they are holding Jack.

"Morning Jack, how are you doing?" I ask as I enter the room.

"Oh, I'm doing loads better Shea. Thank you for everything," he replies.

He sounds chirpier than before, like a weight has been lifted from his shoulders. Jack tells me about his meeting with Vanessa, he tells me how she hugged him so hard they both cried, she told him she forgave him for what he did before and that, with her new family's support, wanted to stay in contact with him.

"That's brilliant news Jack; I'm so pleased for you both. I'm also proud of the progress you're making at the unit. The doctors have said you're doing so well and accepting every therapy session offered, keep it up!" I say to him with a smile.

He smiles just before the usher arrives to show me to the courtroom.

"Remember, let me speak and only speak when spoken to," I say quickly, before leave the room.

He stands up, and gives me a hard salute, "Yes Ma'am," he says, laughing.

I can't help but laugh as I close the door.

I enter the courtroom and dip my head to the Judge.

"Good morning Your Honour," I say.

"Good morning Miss Hopewell, I hope you are prepared for today," replies the Judge. A very serious looking woman with short Grey cropped hair beneath her wig. Her eyes are blue and kind looking despite her serious face.

"I do indeed. I trust you have been fully updated of the circumstances surrounding this case?" I will be acting as prosecution and defence," I state back. I had always been told to be straightforward, to never let your emotions get in the way of your job.

"I am aware. It is a strange case mind you, the fact the defendant wishes for no jury and is willing to accept any sentence passed to him. Let's see how this plays out shall we?" She says, with a hint of humour.

I dip my head again as a sign that I'm ready to start. Everyone begins to file in, Troy followed by Kyron, Vanessa, Linda, Shaun and Skye, follow along behind. I notice that Sierras parents have arrived too. I smile to them out of sympathy, it's my fault their daughter is dead and they are about to find out everything. I wish I could have done something to prepare them for what they are about to hear, but I couldn't.

I wait for the Judge to address the courtroom before they bring Jack in. She reminds everyone that any outbursts from the public gallery will result in him or her being ejected from the court. The Judge then signals for the usher to escort Jack into the dock. I see a tear fall from Skye's eye. She knows everything already but this is the first time she has seen Jack since that night. He refused to see her, I hope it's only because he wants to get better for her.

"Please state your name for the court," the Judge says sternly.

"Jack Woodwin Ma'am," Jack replies clearly, standing straight and facing forward. Jack is ready for this, but something is pestering me inside. Something doesn't feel right.

Chapter 41

We work our way through the facts of the case, working in order of events from oldest to most recent. Jack answers every question honestly and his account is listened to by the Judge, although, contrary to her job title, passes no judgement yet.

"So, Mr Woodwin, you accept that what you did two years ago, kidnapping your daughter and assaulting her mother was against the law?" she asks, in a kind but stern way.

"I do indeed Your Honour," he replies, honestly and clearly.

"Your Honour, Jack has requested an additional charge of harassment be included," I say, holding my head higher to project my voice further.

"For what reason exactly Mr Woodwin?" The Judge directs the question to Jack.

"I sent some rather horrid letters to Miss Summers and to Miss Hopewell. Drunken letters which should never have been written or sent," he replies, again with an honest and clear tone.

"I will consider it," she says thoughtfully. "We will take a short recess before proceeding; I think I need a strong coffee."

We all file out after being dismissed. I head to the vending machine to get something to drink; something is causing me to lose concentration. Troy stops me as I'm just about to choose a latte; I have never drunk latte before.

"Everything alright?" he asks in a worrying tone.

"I'm not sure, something feels off," I reply honestly. "Very off."

Harriet and Lenora sit in the garden admiring the roses. The variety of pinks, reds, and yellows was beyond what Lenora had ever imagined. Jermaine always had the green fingers of the family. She smiled as she remembers him planting the bulbs, watering them lovingly and smiling as they flowered into bright colours.

"Shall we go for a walk?" Lenora asks, lost in a dream world.

"Where are you thinking?" Harriet replies.

"Just a stroll, let's see where we end up," Lenora says, standing up and grabbing her cardigan.

The two women walk arm in arm along the high street, through the nearby park, past the graveyard and on into the fields. Harriet noticed that Lenora had become very pale in her face and seemed to drift off at times; she'd mention it to Shea later.

They walk a little further into the field then they stop to sit down for a while, Lenora lay down in the grass and let herself drift off, Harriet watched her for a few minutes before noticing how shallow her breathing was becoming, she dials an ambulance immediately, all the while trying to wake her best friend.

"Come on Len, you have to wake up, Shea needs you!" Harriet screams through tears. "Come on!"

Harriet gives the call handler their location, who also talks Harriet through CPR if it's needed, Harriet hopes it isn't. After waiting for what feels like hours, Harriet can hear the sirens, so she stands up on her tiptoes to make herself a little taller, waves and shouts as loud as she can to get their attention. As they draw closer, Harriet bends back down to her friend.

"They're here Len, you're going to alright. Come on Len, I just got you back, you can't leave me now!" Harriet cries.

"Could you step back a little madam?" The paramedic asks kindly.

Harriet steps back far enough to give them room to work, but not enough that she loses sight of her sister.

"Any medical history we should know of before we move her?" the second paramedic asks, smiling a kindhearted smile.

"Erm, she has Stage 3 breast cancer," Harriet replies, not taking her eyes on Lenora. "Please help her."

"We will do everything we can. Will you be travelling with us to the hospital?" She asks Harriet.

"Yes, if that's possible, please." Harriet replies with tears flowing down her face. She doesn't attempt to hide them.

The second paramedic helps Harriet into the ambulance before going helping load Lenora in. She sits with them at the back to monitor Lenora. Harriet prays that she will be ok; she watches the slow breaths she is taking. She hasn't asked for God's help since Jemma was drinking but she needed it so desperately now. She hopes He will listen and help.

I begin to walk back to the courtroom when my phone begins to vibrate in my pocket. I know I would only get a phone call if it were urgent as everyone knows where I am today. I pull it out and check the caller ID.

'PRIVATE NUMBER'

I don't miss a beat, I answer the call.

"Hello, Miss Hopewell speaking, how can I help?" I answer, trying to sound professional even though my voice is shaking.

I can hear all sorts of commotion in the background and I really hope I haven't answered a prank call.

"Is this Miss SHEA Hopewell?" The voice from the other end asks, trying to overcome the noise.

"Yes it is, can I ask who you are?" I reply politely.

"My name is Staff Nurse Gregory; we have your mother here, Lenora Hopewell. She was brought in by ambulance less than 10 minutes ago with her friend Harriet Summers. I was told to call you immediately," she replies sympathetically.

"I'm on my way." I say hanging up the phone.

Just as I turn, I collide with Kyron. He looks at me worryingly.

"Are you ok?" he asks quickly.

"No, not really. My Mum is in hospital and I'm stuck here, she has cancer Kyron and I'm terrified!" I say in a hurry.

"Oh, I'm sorry Shea. I'll take you to the hospital in a patrol car. I'll get Troy to ask for a postponement on personal grounds. Let's go!" he says, pulling his phone out at the same time.

We get in the car and he puts the sirens on to rush me there. It's unethical but he can see how upset I am.

"I hope she alright, please let her be alright, don't take her yet, I'm not ready to let her go," I let myself whisper. I feel a soft squeeze of my shoulder and I know Zephyr is there with me.

Chapter 42

"The Judge has granted a 3 day adjournment on personal ground, she also sends her best wishes to your Mum," Kyron says, reading from his phone.

We are in the waiting room on the emergency department waiting for the doctor to come out of Mum's room. I can't stop pacing the floor; I've probably made this part of the floor cleaner than the rest!

"Sit down love, you're no good to her like this," Harriet says softly.

"I wish I could just sit down, but Mum has been looking really ill lately, and all this has taken its toll on her, I'm sure of it. It's all my fault!" I say, sobbing into Harriets shoulder.

"Now now dear, none of this is anyone's fault so stop that talk. Look the doctor is coming over." She says, patting my hair.

I look up to find a solemn looking doctor walking towards us, he has a serious face with light brown eyes and a generous amount of salt and pepper coloured hair. His face gives nothing away but I look at him with hope and need. I need Mum to be alright, I hope he has an answer.

"Its touch and go I'm afraid," he says, looking into my eyes.

"How long?" I ask I know he means the cancer has spread; I don't need it spelt out for me.

"We really don't want to estimate a time frame, I wouldn't want to," he says sympathetically. "I would suggest spending as much time as possible with her."

"Thank you doctor. Thank you for your honesty and your time," I say, shaking his hand.

"Hello, Summers household?" Derek says, picking up the phone.

"Derek, it's me, you need to come to the hospital, room 207, second floor. Its Len," Harriet says in a hurry.

"What's happened?" he asks putting his shoes on as he speaks.

"It's not looking good darling, not good at all. I'll see you when you get here," she says and then hangs up.

Derek prays the whole way to the hospital, he prays for Len, for Shea and for Harriet. He prays that, if it is her time to go, that she leaves in a peaceful way, without pain or anguish and that she be accepted into Heaven, which is where she belonged. He knew Shea was a strong girl, but she would need them both is Len did pass. "Please let her live," he prayed. "If only for a while longer."

He arrives at the hospital at the same time as Troy. Troy had worked with Jermaine and felt an obligation to be there for Lenora and Shea.

"Thank you for coming," Derek says with tears in his eyes.

Troy had no words to say, just a solemn smile as he gestures Derek to lead the way.

Seeing Mum laying there helpless and frail broke my heart to pieces. Kyron guides me to her bedside slowly and sits me down on the chair next to her bed. I have no idea what to do or say, I hold her hand and stroke her arm, just like she used to do with me when I was scared. Harriet rests her hand gently on my shoulder; I can hear her soft cries. I try to hate her for causing so much stress on Mum with this twin sister thing but I can't, it means so much to her. Kyron ushers Harriet out so I can be alone with Mum.

"Hey Mum," I say as they close the door. "I'm here, I don't know what to do Mum. I need you."

I can feel the air in the room shift slightly.

"How is she?" A voice asks beside me.

"Oh, Zephyr, It's not looking good," I cry, trying to sound stronger than I'm feeling but inside I'm breaking to bits.

"I'm sorry Shea. She's a good one, your Mum," he replies.

It shocks me a little as that is so similar to what my Dad used to say, but it's a common thing to say.

I look around to him but he's gone. I look back at Mum and feel the air shift again, this time Zephyr hasn't come back. Mum's chest rises and slowly falls. I watch for the next breath, willing her chest to rise and fall again but it doesn't. I can't scream, I can't speak, I can hardly breathe, I let the tears fall silently. I don't let go of her hand, I know she's gone. I felt it, but I need to hold on a little longer, she's still there, somewhere.

I hear the door open and close softly behind me but I don't turn to see who is there. I can't face anyone right now. I feel a heavy hand rest on my shoulder, its one I have felt before. The same one I felt when we were told about Dad. I know it's Troy. I turn to him, my face red and swollen from crying, he doesn't say a word, just bows his head telling me he understands what has happened.

"I'll be outside when you're ready," he says as he turns to leave.

I can't speak, I don't even try, I just nod letting the tears fall silently. Troy must have informed everyone outside because I can hear Harriet wailing. How am I supposed to carry on now? I'm not even sure what time it is, I don't even know what to do now. I gather myself together; give Mum one last kiss on the head.

"Have a safe journey Mum, I love you. Look after her Dad; she's coming back to you." I say as I look up. I don't know if I'm hearing things but I swear I heard Dad say he will, but I shake my head and put it down to shock and grief.

As I leave the side room, I signal to the doctors that she has gone, not wanting to wait around while they prepare her for the morgue. I link arms with Troy and we leave the hospital, leave Harriet wailing, and leave Derek looking stunned and Kyron looking sympathetic. I don't need that right now. I need to compose myself, I need to grieve. Troy drives me home in silence. He looks over once or twice but doesn't speak. He opens my door when we stop.

"You know how to reach me, at any time," he says, giving me a hug.

I can't speak so I just give a curt nod. I turn and go inside, the warmth gathering me into an embrace. I slide to the floor and break down, alone in my childhood home.

Chapter 43

It's been 3 days since I lost Mum, but it really feels like it's just happened. I've had messages, cards, flowers and meals sent to me. You never truly realise that when people say 'it takes a village to raise a child' they actually mean it. Troy has been great; his wife is an amazing cook. It's time for me to pull myself together and face the world once again though. This is for you Mum.

"Ready kid?" Troy asks playfully as I join him at the end of Mum's driveway.

laugh at him and swat at his arm.

"On a serious note, are you sure you're ready?" he asks, straightening himself up.

"I have to do this. I promised Jack and I promised Mum I'd see it through," I reply, smiling when I remember Mum making me promise.

Troy nods politely and gestures to the waiting car. I gather myself and climb in. It's time to face the music. I just hope we are all singing from the same hymn sheet!

The courtroom is quiet whilst we await the Judge's arrival. I quickly survey the room. Harriet and Derek are sitting, huddled together. I must remember to catch up with them afterwards. I haven't spoken to either of them since Mum passed. I can see Skye at the back; it looks like she is saying a prayer. Mr and Mrs Jackson are just next to her. I wish they hadn't had to hear all that about Sierra, I hope it has brought them some form of closure.

"All rise!" the usher demands, shaking me from my thoughts.

The Judge enters the room and looks around, she catches my eye.

"Deepest condolences Miss Hopewell. Are you sure you are ready to continue?" She asks kindly.

"Thank you Your Honour. Yes I am indeed ready to continue," I reply with a courteous nod.

She nods back and takes her place.

I look at Jack who has his head bowed. It's time to begin. As I am about to speak I hear the door open and close behind me.

"Sorry we're late Ma'am," Shaun announces as he ushers Vanessa to a seat.

"Apology accepted, please be seated." She says with a small smile.

I clear my throat and begin my statement.

"As you can see Your Honour, my client has lived with an undiagnosed mental illness for his entire life, with no help from family or friends. He has come to terms with what he has done and is willing to accept the sentence handed to him. All he asks is that he remains in contact with his daughter, Vanessa," I say, gesturing to Vanessa seated next to Skye and Shaun.

The Judge nods her head towards me.

"Jack is progressing well with the help of the secure unit he is currently being held in. The doctors say he is responding well to the sessions available to him and has even volunteered for extra sessions. It is my understanding that he has taken on board what the police have told him and is no longer a threat. I rest my case." I say, ending my statement.

"Is all that has been said and recorded the whole truth?" She asks Jack directly.

"Yes Ma'am," Jack responds politely. "Complete truth."

"Do you wish to address the court Mr Woodwin?" she asks.

"If I may Your Honour," he says nervously.

He turns to face the public gallery.

"I am deeply sorry for all the pain and grief I have caused. If I could turn the hands of time back, I would. Mr and Mrs Jackson, I deeply apologise for what I did to Sierra, she was a beautiful young lady," he says with tears falling from his eye.

"You are forgiven Mr Woodwin; we understand that it was an accident. May the Lord guide you through the rest of your life and keep you on the right path," they say, wiping their eyes.

The Judge composes herself after Jack's emotional speech.

"I will reside to my chambers to consider a sentence to coincide with the charges brought against you. We will reconvene is 2 hours," she says sternly.

"All rise," the usher announces again.

The judge leaves the room, Jack is taken away and the public gallery files out, I follow along behind.

"Shea?"

I turn to see Mr and Mrs Jackson behind me.

"I'm sorry you had to listen to all of that," I say, wishing I had better words for them.

"Not at all, it was just the closure we needed, Sierra can finally Rest In Peace," Mr Jackson says, shaking my hand. "But we must be going now, please inform us of the outcome and our deepest condolences for the loss of your Mum."

"I certainly will and thank you," I say as they head out of the court building doors. I smile as I watch them leave.

Kyron hands me a polystyrene cup of tea, hot with lots of sugar.

"Thank," I say, taking a sip, the heat warms me like a hug.

Idle chitchat passes between us all. Unsure of what to say or how to act, I try to keep myself distant. I watch as Harriet and Derek take to Vanessa like their own grandchild, sad to think Mum will never see grandchildren, guilty I never gave her any.

"If you would kindly return to the court, the Judge has reached her decision," The usher announces.

I glance at the clock, it's only been an hour, sometimes this can be a blessing, sometimes a curse.

"All rise."

The Judge returns to her seat and looks directly at Jack, who stands nervously with his hands clasped in front of him. I feel sick to my stomach waiting for her to speak.

"With all the evidence presented to me today and at the last hearing, I am endeavoured to pass sentence of you Mr Jack Woodwin," she begins. "There are mitigating circumstances and I must take into account your remorse and the victim impact statements presented to me. I hereby sentence you to 15 years imprisonment, you are to serve half your sentence in the secure unit to aid with you impairment, the second half to be determined at your next hearing in seven and a half years time, this is all dependant on your progress between now and then," she says, slamming her gavel down.

Everyone lets out a breath. Jack nods his acceptance, he understand, he is ready to make amends.

Chapter 44

It's been a week since Mum's funeral. Harriet and Derek have been there for me, helping me plan every detail. Family and friends arrived from all over the world to say goodbye. I'm slowly learning to grieve for Mum, Dad, and Jemma. I have received flowers from Mr and Mrs Jackson. They sent a note to say they are in contact with Jack. They believe they can help him, I believe they just might be able to.

As I finish packing up the rest of the things for storage, I find a picture of Mum, Dad and I taken in The Seychelles over 15 years ago.

"I miss you both," I say, holding the picture close. I hope you have found each other. Keep watch over me."

I let some tears fall as I replace an old photo of Mum and

Harriet with a newer one. I've decided to stay in Leeds and

continue my career up here. I think it was meant to be.

Getting up from the floor, I head down to the kitchen to tidy up the breakfast stuff. Lana and Louis had come with cookies; I can still smell them now. I smile as I rinse up the cups, looking out towards the roses. Dad loved his garden. I hope I can keep it going. I open the cupboard and place the plates and cups away, spending a few minutes looking at Mums cup next to Dads, never to be used again, but always to be looked after. I close the cupboard door and almost drop the bowl I'm holding.

"Zephyr! You scared me!" I say, clutching my chest.

"Ha-ha! Here I am!" he laughs. "I wanted to check on you. Lovely service by the way, your Mum would be proud."

"Thanks. I'm doing alright. I still miss her though. It's going to take time," I say, wiping a tear from my eye.

"I know it will," he replies with a smile. "You will get there."

I smile back. I can see him fading away. I prepare myself for life alone. He saved me from everything. I look back towards the kitchen door and see Zephyr there, with Mum! He has his arm around her waist. He winks at me as Mum smiles the sweetest, most peaceful smile.

"Dad?" I whisper.

He slowly fades away, taking Mum with him.

THE END

Printed in Great Britain
by Amazon